HATS OFF TO LOVE

Denise had landed her dream job at 'Something Special' fashion boutique . . . until an accident put paid to her start date. When her new hobby grew into a small business, her boss, shop owner Craig, was willing to lend his full support. So why was work colleague Jeannie so jealous? He was a free man. In Paris at the fashion weekend, Craig revealed his intentions. Denise knew she had to leave. Like the delicate butterfly on Sadie's roses, love always escaped her . . .

SUSAN JONES

HATS OFF TO LOVE

Complete and Unabridged

LINFORD
Leicester

First published in Great Britain in 2016

First Linford Edition
published 2020

A catalogue record for this book is available
from the British Library.

ISBN 978–1–4448–4626–3

Published by
Ulverscroft Limited
Anstey, Leicestershire
Set by Words & Graphics Ltd.
Anstey, Leicestershire
Printed and bound in Great Britain by
TJ Books Limited, Padstow, Cornwall

This book is printed on acid-free paper

1

Denise Gambon caught her breath as wind sent her golden hair swirling around her face. Securing stray wisps, she turned the corner from Canal Walk and made her way up into Mullsey High Street.

As it was a Wednesday, not a market day, she was able to take the short cut across the market square. She'd spotted the advertisement in the window of Something Special, the recently opened dress shop, two days earlier. Rather than go in unprepared, she'd written down the number, taken it home and then made the call. Now she was ready to face the interview.

Her confident walk hid any sign of nerves that may have been lurking. Quickly taking a sideways glance in the window of the phone shop reassured Denise that the knee-length vintage dress in forest green she'd chosen, with its pretty lacy collar, made her look slimmer than she actually was. The brown boots she wore added a few inches to her height, and confidence as well.

They wanted a sales assistant for every Saturday and a couple of evenings. That would still give her time to complete her textiles and design course at college. What had begun as a hobby had turned into an absorbing interest in fashion and clothing trends.

She really wanted to work in this exciting new shop — so much more interesting than a huge chain store where everything was the same, whichever town you happened to be in.

Denise hitched her tan leather bag up her arm, then flicked her hair over her shoulder and opened the shop door. A waft of jasmine and roses drifted through the warm air. Her amber eyes glowed with flecks of gold as she caught the attention of the smartly dressed older lady behind the counter, busy arranging stockings and tights on a display rack.

'I've come for an interview.' She smiled. 'I'm Denise Gambon — were you the lady I spoke with on the phone?'

'Ah, Denise — that's right, we did. I'm Maud. Hang on a moment, and I'll give him a shout.' She disappeared through a door at the back of the shop.

Denise glanced round at the fashions with fingers crossed behind her back. She hoped there hadn't been many enquiries; for her this would be a dream job.

She admired a crochet dress with matching hat, displayed artistically on a side wall of the shop. Dark peach wouldn't be a colour she'd choose for herself, but she could imagine a dark-haired woman wearing it for a day out in the summer . . .

'Hello. You've come about the vacancy?'

Jolted from her dreams of a summer day, Denise turned to look into the face

3

of Craig Spencer.

Dark curls, which looked to have a mind of their own, framed a tanned face. The blue of his eyes reminded her of a kingfisher she'd watched, diving for fish on one of her many walks along the canal. Any idea of what she had planned to say escaped her.

He offered his hand, and gave her a smile which immediately put her at ease.

'I'm Craig Spencer, and you're Denise, Maud tells me.' He turned and nodded to Maud, who was now dusting a shelf.

'I'll get these handbags out on show. I was thinking of putting them on here, if that's alright with you, Craig.' Maud had a pile of varying shades of bags to her side in readiness. 'Would you like some tea bringing through?'

'Only if you have time, Maud, thanks. We'll have a chat in my office. This way.'

He led Denise through the shop and upstairs to where he opened the door to a light, airy room with huge windows.

'I've seen a few people for the job so far. This is the last day of interviews.' He smiled and sat down behind a desk, indicating a chair opposite for Denise.

'Oh, I see.' Denise's heart sank as she wondered if he had someone in mind already.

'So, are you working anywhere at the moment?' He studied her with those deep blue eyes, and she hoped the words wouldn't get stuck in her throat. Already her palms were becoming sticky and her heart was beating a bit faster than normal.

'No, I'm at college, studying textiles and design. I'd be really interested in working here.'

'It's a part-time job we're offering.' He leaned forward and scribbled in a notebook that lay in front of him. 'Maud will have explained that I'm looking for someone who can cover two evenings as well.'

'She did tell me that, yes.' Denise nodded and hoped she didn't look over-eager. 'I'm available to cover those times. I saw the advert in the window.'

Craig sat back and looked thoughtful.

'I've sorted out my ladies who cover the days. Maud, you've already met, and then there's another two who help out as well, Jeanie and Linda. I've got my team, only the Saturday girl to put in place. Everyone wants a job with no evening or weekend work.' Craig laughed lightly.

Denise batted her eyes quickly, knowing this was her only chance to speak up, even if it meant repeating herself.

'I'm the opposite. I know I'd really enjoy working here, and it's only a short walk from where I live, along the canal. Our cottage — well, my landlady Sadie's cottage — backs onto the canal. I only have to come over the bridge and up Canal Walk.'

Craig smiled. 'You're a lodger? Where do your family live — anywhere near?'

That was one question she hoped

wouldn't come up.

'There was a boating accident, a few years ago now. I really don't like to talk about it.'

She looked up and met his gaze.

Denise breathed more easily when he shook his dark curls and said, 'That's understandable, sorry to hear about that. Next question is . . . What's that extra something you'd bring to our business that nobody else could?'

Craig threw his pen across his desk and sat upright, took a deep breath and clasped his palms, waiting for her reply.

Clearing her throat, Denise gave a shy smile and began, 'I really want to work in your shop, as I've always had an interest in fashion. I like to find something different, which I think your shop is.' She checked to see whether he was still listening. 'Not that I've ever been to a Paris fashion show or anything like that.' Denise laughed nervously. She had to say something right now; it was her last chance to make an impression.

'I'm, um, approachable, friendly and I like to think I've got an eye for something that works. I would help make the shop a success. Maybe if you agreed, I could organise fashion shows and themed evenings. Vintage is taking off now as well, and I'd love a chance to promote that side of fashion which I feel is often overlooked.'

Denise stopped short. She had been rambling. Maybe overstepped the mark, she couldn't tell.

Craig gave a slow smile, and tilted his head.

'Where did you buy the dress you're wearing today?'

She was jolted from the impact of such a personal question.

'What, this old thing?' Denise gave a self-conscious laugh and tugged at the green velvet dress, looking down at her hand-made creation. 'I've had it for some time. Is that a usual question asked at the interview?'

He was surely making fun? There was no way she was going to admit that the

8

green velvet had previously made perfectly good curtains in her family home.

'No, I only wondered. It's different, like you.' He smiled.

From the determined twinkle in his eye, he genuinely seemed to want to know, so she plumped for an honest reply.

'It's something I designed myself and with a bit of help it turned out wearable, I think.'

Denise prayed he didn't ask any more questions as to how long ago she'd made it. Her mother had shown her how to attach the lacy collar and she always called it her 'lucky dress'.

'It certainly is 'wearable'.' He raised his eyebrows and silence followed. Craig doodled on the pad in front of him, appearing to disappear into his thoughts, and then he spoke.

'I'd like to offer you the job, Denise. You'll complement the others, and get on well with them all, I hope. Can you start this Saturday?'

Denise knew it wouldn't be appropriate to jump over the desk and throw her arms round his neck, so with a superhuman effort she smiled calmly and replied, 'Mr Spencer, thank you so much. That's fantastic.' She could feel her whole body shaking with excitement and hoped it didn't show.

She'd got the job — and so quickly as well! Her cheeks felt flushed and she imagined she looked hot and flustered, but she didn't care. Her savings from her parents' legacy had been dwindling. Now she'd be able to get back on her feet and treat her lovely landlady to something special on payday.

As she was wondering how to bring up the subject of wages, Craig told her about the three-month trial period, and that from a basic wage, pay would increase according to how she went on. Denise vowed silently that she'd put all her efforts into being the best sales assistant at Something Special.

'We'll see you on Saturday, then — half past eight start.'

A brief knock was followed by Maud entering with a tray holding teapot with two cups, milk and sugar, a welcome sight.

'Denise is our new recruit.' He spoke to Maud, and then swung round to face Denise. 'You'll have one of us with you all the time and mostly it's a matter of displaying stock to the best advantage, and people skills. Thanks for that, Maud.'

Denise's new colleague turned to go and smiled broadly in her direction. 'That's good news — congratulations. I told him you sounded polite and friendly on the phone.'

Glad of the tea to calm the shakes from the anticipation she was feeling, Denise finished her cup and scooped up her bag that lay by her feet.

Craig walked her to the door and it was only when Denise had turned the corner into Canal Walk that she breathed a sigh of relief.

She lifted her face skyward and let the breeze ruffle her hair all it liked.

Her face broke into a smile that grew until she couldn't stop the laughter that bubbled up from her chest and out into the open for anyone who might be listening. Only there was nobody around as she made her way along the canal tow path, apart from a cluster of ducks paddling along.

'I did it! Yes! I got the job.'

The warmth of afternoon sunshine came bursting through, as if to celebrate with her. She began doing a little dance, then a twirl. As she began singing, a voice drifted over the hedge.

'Glad someone's happy.' The gardener stuck his spade in the ground and popped his head over the iron gate. 'What's put the smile on your face today, then? Won the lottery or something?' His craggy face, weathered from most weekends on the allotments, gave Joe the look of someone well-travelled. His mother lived next door to them and was Sadie's oldest friend.

Bursting to tell someone her good

news, Denise was glad to chat for a while.

'I got the job, in that new dress shop in Mullsey High Street, Joe. You know the one?'

Joe frowned, pursing his lips and turning eyes to the side as if searching for a cryptic clue.

'Mm, no, can't say as I've heard of it. Our Vera will have, though. What's it called?'

'Something Special, and it really is, Joe — all unique dresses and the handbags! You've never seen such colours and designs. I've already seen one I'd like.'

Joe chuckled. 'Sounds to me like you'll be spending half your wages in there. They've made a wise move, employing you. You'll finish college this year, then?'

'That's right, when I've finished my exams and the bonus is, well . . . ' Denise didn't have any words, only an enormous smile. 'Let's say it's the best news I've had in ages.'

'Good luck to you, time you had a bit of luck, what with all that, you know . . . Hey, and talking of good news, I've been offered early retirement. I've said yes.' Joe stood tall, stretching to his full five feet eight inches and ruffling his thatch of blond hair that was greying at the sides. 'Vera's happy about it, and I've had a good payout. Time to give the youngsters a chance, Denise, that's the thing.'

'You'll have more time for the allotment then, Joe?' Denise leaned on the gate and looked across to where he'd dug and planted one plot and was starting on another.

'Aye, I applied for another, they've said yes, so that'll keep me busy, and out of Vera's way.' He gave Denise a wink, and picked up his spade then turned to carry on with his work. 'Say hello to Sadie from me.'

Denise called after his retreating back, 'I will — see you around, Joe.'

Forgetting about happy dancing, she walked as quickly as she could — not easy in those boots, but soon she was making her way across the bridge and into the cutting that led to Sadie's back garden. The gate gave its usual squeak, and she walked up the crazy paving pathway and through the back door. A waft of warm cottage pie-scented air met her as she entered the kitchen, reminding her how hungry she was.

Denise called up the stairs, 'Sadie, it's me! I've got some news, are you there?'

The house was surprisingly quiet. Opening the front door, Denise checked the garden. Often Sadie could be found on her hands and knees, pulling up weeds that grew faster than the flowers, she always said.

A glance up the street. Still no sign.

Denise nipped down the front path and went next door to where Celia Clarke lived. Knocking briefly on the front door, she tried the handle. Open as usual. She let herself in.

'Celia, are you there?'

It was Sadie who replied.

15

'Denise, you're back! Thank goodness for that. It's Celia, she tripped over that bit of loose carpet and fell down the stairs. Luckily she had her mobile in her pocket and called me. I didn't want to leave her in case she passed out.'

Sadie was sitting on the floor beside Celia, stroking her hand, and pressing a cold flannel to her head.

'Has she had any tea or anything to drink?' Denise sat beside the two elderly ladies. 'I've just been talking to Joe — he's on the allotment, Celia.' She smiled gently at Celia who was looking slightly embarrassed.

'I'll be alright, didn't want to make a fuss. It hurts when I try to move, that's all.'

'I'll get her some tea, Denise — you stay with her a while. Thought it best not to try and move her until someone's checked everything.'

Sadie bustled to the kitchen and soon they heard the clattering of mugs and spoons stirring plenty of sugar into the drinks.

When she reappeared, Denise spoke gently to Celia.

'Listen, I'm going to run back along the canal and fetch Joe — he'll be able to help us move you onto the settee. Sadie, we really ought to ring for an ambulance.'

Celia looked about to cry. Denise forced herself to be practical and not waste time.

'I'll be as quick as I can, promise.'

Giving Sadie her mobile after tapping in the number for Mullsey General Hospital, she nipped next door and changed into her old jeans and trainers. Remembering to switch the oven off — the shepherd's pie smelt well and truly baked — she retraced her steps and then sprinted along the canal tow path.

She could see the stooped back of Joe, engrossed in planting something that looked like potatoes. Denise put one foot on the bottom bar of the gate, and held onto the top. She heaved herself up, and pushed her weight onto her hands to launch herself over it, shouting his name at the same time.

'Joe, it's your mum! Joe . . . ' Her words were lost in the breeze as she performed an ungainly somersault, which ended up with her landing with a thud on the other side of the gate, her foot wedged between the bars as she fell.

* * *

Denise knew her leg didn't feel right. Every time she tried to move it, she felt a knife jabbing up through her ankle. Her head began to pound and she felt quite ill. When Joe's face appeared above her, she remembered why she'd dived like some crazy girl over an old rusty gate.

'Your mum — she's fallen and an ambulance is on its way.'

'Looks like she's not the only one. Can you stand?' He grasped her arm, and pulled her to a standing position after gently releasing her foot from where it was twisted around the metal bar.

'Ow, ow, ow! Let me stand on my own. Why didn't I stay over that side?' Denise looked angrily at the old gate that was kept padlocked. Gingerly she placed the right foot down on to the grass. When she tried to walk, her leg buckled underneath her weight. 'Oh, Joe, you go to your mum — I'll just wait a while.'

'You need to get that looked at from what I can see. Hang on tight.' With a deft movement, Joe gently pulled Denise over his shoulder and carefully negotiated the gate while holding on to her knees. 'Keep still and we'll be there in a flash.'

Holding on for dear life and hardly daring to breathe in case she put him off his stride and ended up in the canal, Denise grasped Joe's thick jumper and watched the ground whizzing past as he moved like a man much younger than his fifty-nine years.

Joe placed Denise down gently in his

mother's living room where the paramedics were making checks on Celia.
All heads turned when Denise gasped
and lifted her swollen ankle up onto the
footstool.

'Denise, you look a fright. You were
only supposed to fetch Joe, not come
back needing a doctor. Are you alright?'
Sadie immediately gathered cushions
for Denise to lean on and pulled the
throw from the back of Celia's armchair
to cover her knees.

'Ow, it hurts . . . ' Denise cried out
when she looked down at her foot.
Then put her hand to her head. 'I feel
such a fool and I'm in agony.'

The two paramedics, satisfied that
Celia would be alright after some rest,
turned their attention to the new
patient.

'Handy we were here, then,' one
quipped. They touched and probed
while Denise yelped and screamed.

'We'll have to take you in for x-rays
and to see the doctor with that. Have
you got an overnight bag? You might

have to stay in if it's broken.'

Denise was shocked into silence. They busily filled in paperwork, and made preparations to move her to Mullsey General.

'I'll go and put a few things ready for you,' Sadie said. 'I can't believe it, such a silly thing to happen, after you'd been for your interview and I've made your favourite for tea.'

Denise noticed Sadie's deep frown lines.

'I'm sorry to worry you — I'd got some great news as well.' Struggling to sit upright among the many pillows that Sadie had arranged around her, Denise licked her dry lips. 'I got the job, Sadie, I start on Saturday.'

'This Saturday, you mean?' Sadie sucked on her lower lip and glanced at Denise's ankle. 'That looks like it's getting bigger to me.' She frowned again.

Realisation dawned; Denise smacked her hand on the throw over that Sadie had used to keep her warm.

'Blow and blast, this might not be right by then . . . Oh no. I have to go, even if it means hobbling in.' Lower lip quivering, she closed her eyes and wished the pain would go away.

'Tell you what, give them a ring and explain. Surely they'll understand, it's an accident — not as if you got yourself in that state on purpose, now, is it?'

Sadie passed Denise her mobile off the sideboard, and bustled off to pack her bag.

'It's only just happened. I fell off a gate . . . ' Trying to ignore the constant throbbing that persisted in her right ankle, Denise nodded into her phone.

The paramedics were aligning a temporary stretcher alongside where she sat. Trying to hurry the phone call that she'd dreaded making, Denise closed her eyes in frustration.

'I feel such an idiot — it's the way I fell. No, not sure, they'll be able to tell me if it's broken when I've had x-rays. Just wanted to let you know in case they keep me in, and it's only two days until

I should be starting.'

Sadie hovered by the door with a small pink bag. She held it up and nodded to where the ambulance driver was looking agitated.

'I'm sorry to rush off, Mr Spencer, but the ambulance is waiting. I'll let you know how I get on.' Denise closed her eyes and wished this nightmare of an afternoon could be a distant memory. 'That's really good of you, thanks, it means a lot.' Switching the phone off, she turned to Sadie. 'He said the job is still there for me. I can take as long as I need.'

Her eyes felt blurry as she was carried down the pathway. It was only when she could no longer see Sadie waving, and they closed the back door to the ambulance that Denise felt tears begin to spill onto her cheeks.

2

Craig Spencer cleared a space on his desk and placed his morning coffee down on the old leather place mat. He enjoyed this quiet time, checking through latest stock deliveries, catching up with emails, and planning his day before the shop was open.

Fresh from the shower, his damp curls brushed his collar. He usually wore a white or pale blue shirt for work, teamed with stone washed chinos. He leaned on the thick stone wall that framed the large window.

Watching Mullsey High Street come alive usually captivated him; only today, a girl with flyaway golden hair was on his mind. She'd made an enthusiastic pitch for the job, mainly the reason he'd made the rash decision to offer it to her immediately — something he'd never done.

Now after sleeping on it, he wondered if it might be a decision he'd regret. Either she was accident-prone, or someone who went charging over gates like an acrobat, without a care for what was on the other side. He smiled to himself then shook his head free from thoughts of a girl with amber eyes whom he'd only just met.

He took a drink of his coffee, and switched on the laptop. Quickly scanning emails, nothing looked urgent; he'd reply to those later. Now he was still without a Saturday girl, and she could be off for a week or two. He had full confidence in his staff, whom he'd known a long while. They'd take turns to cover. Maud was a friend of his mother, while Linda and Jeanie had worked for him in his previous business.

Craig had a to-do list that was mounting. He'd considered getting help in the office, but then changed his mind. Whenever the phone rang, it was always him people wanted to speak to.

He liked making decisions, being his own man; the hard work was paying off now he'd moved into the better end of fashion and had the chance to open the shop, though he'd always be glad of those teenage years on the market. There he'd learned all he knew about buying and selling.

When Denise joined the team, he'd get her to help with emails and phone calls if he needed a hand. She'd be more up to date with technology than the others.

There he was, thinking about her again . . .

A glance at the clock told him Maud would be arriving in the next ten minutes. He shut down the computer and went down to unlock the door.

Predictably five minutes early, Maud breezed in with her usual waft of floral scent — Estée Lauder, Beautiful — he knew because she kept a bottle under the counter.

'Morning, Craig. Looks like it might

clear up later. Time the weather changed for the better.'

Craig glanced up from where he was flicking through the order book.

'Hello, Maud, I know, especially with all these arriving. More on the way as well.' He nodded to where a row of bright coloured summer dresses hung waiting to be snapped up. 'There's more of the maxi style coming later, ready for the weekend.'

'They're lovely. We had a customer in last week, I think I told you. She wanted something for a cruise holiday, asking when we'd be having some in. She'll be pleased.'

Maud went through her morning rituals — handbag tucked into the cupboard in the kitchen, kettle on, scarf and jacket hung on the peg behind the door, and then arranging bags and tissue paper ready for wrapping whatever was sold on this Thursday morning.

'It'll be nice for Denise to be able to arrange those then when she starts on

Saturday. We'll keep an eye on her at first, of course.'

'Yes, that's what I was about to tell you.' Craig walked between racks of clothing, flicking through a range of short pastel jackets as he spoke. 'She's had a fall . . . over a gate, went off to hospital yesterday, so it might be the following week, or even the one after that. I told her to call in when she's ready to start.'

Craig ran his hand across the back of his neck. Maud had a habit of saying things as they were. He waited for some comment like, *You were a bit too hasty there*.

'She seemed like a lively girl. I hope she does come back — oh well, never mind, we'll manage until she's better. It can't take that long to recover from — a fall, did you say? And what was she doing on a gate?' Maud sent a look across the counter that gave Craig cause to chuckle.

'I wondered the same. A lively girl, as you'd noticed.' He returned to his office, leaving Maud to do what she did best.

* * *

It had been a long night, visiting the x-ray department and then seeing a nurse, a junior doctor and then a specialist who had wrapped her ankle in a plaster cast.

'To keep the joint protected, while the sprain heals,' the doctor had told her.

Glad of the painkillers that had worked a miracle, Denise was convinced she'd be better off at home, and swung her legs out of the bed and stood up.

'Argh!' Slumping to the floor in a heap, she bit on her lower lip to stop from screaming out. The painkillers had made her forget how bad the injury was. There was no way she'd be walking properly for a while. She'd momentarily forgotten about her foot being in plaster.

The dark-haired nurse was beside her in moments. 'That's what you get for trying to escape.' She smiled and helped Denise back into bed. 'It won't be long, and then the doctor will give you the all-clear, hopefully, eh?'

Denise nodded and gave her a half smile back.

It seemed like hours later when her lunch of steamed fish with vegetables arrived. The meal wasn't a patch on Sadie's cooking, but she ate, glad of something to distract her.

'You'll be glad to hear there are no broken bones.' Doctor Malik held up the x-ray and showed Denise the area that had been badly sprained. 'Keep taking the painkillers and rest as much as possible. Bruising is to be expected, and having the plaster over it will help the ligaments to heal quicker.'

'I'm supposed to be starting a new job. Will it take long to repair?' Denise held her breath, hoping to hear him say a few days.

'Could be a few weeks, usually three

to four, or even up to three months if you don't rest. I would advise you to walk on it at least two or three times a day, but only a few steps. What kind of work are you going to be doing?'

When Denise explained it was shop work, he shook his head.

'No, I'll sign a sick note for three weeks, and you'll need to come back and see me in a week to change the cast for you. After that, your GP will advise.' Scribbling on the clipboard, Dr Malik added, 'You can go home, but make sure you listen to all the advice Sister Morgan gives you.'

He moved on to the next bed, leaving Denise grappling for her mobile.

★　★　★

'It was really good of Joe to come and get me.' Denise winced as she adjusted her foot on the huge stool in Sadie's living room.

'He said he would.' Sadie picked up her knitting and levelled the stitches on her needles as she spoke. 'You'd still be there now if it meant waiting for an ambulance, and a taxi would have cost a fortune.'

'I offered to give him petrol money, but he wouldn't take any.' Denise sighed and thumped her arm on the side of the chair. 'I feel useless, sitting here and this could go on for weeks. I doubt Craig Spencer will keep the job open that long for me. I might as well forget it.'

Sadie peered over her glasses.

'It's no use feeling sorry for yourself. There's a lot worse off than you. Why don't you give your friend a call? What's her name, that girl who you went swimming with last week?'

'Think I will.' Denise jabbed at her phone. Texting her friend was easier than talking and she wasn't in the mood to be chirpy. All she wanted was to be planning what she'd wear for her first day at the shop.

Sadie was right, though; this was a minor hitch in the grand scheme of things. She opened the huge footstool that doubled as a craft box, and found a pack of pastels. There were a couple of sketch pads in there beside them.

Doodling at first and then drawing what she imagined being the perfect outfit, her sadness lifted. Only when Sadie handed her a hot chocolate did she realise the evening had flown by.

★ ★ ★

Hobbling to the kitchen and back to the living room was the most Denise could manage for the first couple of days. The phone call to Something Special had been easier than she thought. It was Linda who'd answered the phone on the Friday.

'I'm the new Saturday girl — just to let you know, I'm home from hospital, but they've told me to rest for a couple of weeks.' Denise crossed her fingers and cringed at the sound of her fibs. She was only slightly flustered when Linda had put Craig on the line.

'What's the verdict?' she heard his deep voice asking.

'Nothing's broken, and it should be fine in a week or two — three at the most.' She didn't want to make false promises. He was being much too fair for that. 'Maybe I could come in and sit down in-between . . .'

He didn't let her finish the sentence.

'Absolutely not; we only want you back here when you're fit enough to run up those stairs, and jog up to the cake shop on Saturday mornings. Is that clear?' His abrupt tone with obvious jokes made her giggle, and she knew the job would be hers as soon as she was better.

'Thank you. I'll keep in touch.' She frowned at her familiar tone. Up until the other day she'd never met him. Now she was speaking as if she were one of the team.

Still, if anyone was being familiar, it was Craig. She imagined his curls falling around his forehead and wondered if he was wearing the same white shirt, with the top few buttons open, that he had worn the other day.

'Good stuff, talk soon, bye.'

Denise looked at the phone as if it had sizzled. He'd rung off like a man on a mission. Then again, he was — on a mission to run his shop and take lots of money. That's what businessmen did, she had to remind herself. He was probably quite annoyed and he was covering it well.

She smiled a half-smile to herself, and didn't realise Sadie was standing by the kitchen door watching her.

'All sorted, then?' She raised an eyebrow.

The brisk knock at the back door made them both jump.

'Who's that? Come on in, don't stand there.'

Only friends and people they knew used the back door, by going along the passageway at the side of the house. Mostly Sadie and Denise lived in the back part of the house, where the kitchen and living room were kept heated. The front lounge was used more at the weekend.

'Oh, your friend's here now. Come on in, love.'

Beulah Struthers appeared. She had rosy cheeks and her sparkling blueygrey eyes flicked anxiously from one to the other.

'Is this a good time? Only I've got the day off college and thought I'd pop round to see the invalid.' She glanced down at the thick plaster that covered Denise's right foot. 'Does it hurt?' Looking from the foot to Denise's face, she grimaced. 'Silly question, of course it does. Anything I can do?' She looked quite helpless and a bit embarrassed, clearly relieved when Sadie sent them off to sit down.

'You go into the other room, I'll get some tea and toast on the go,' she said briskly.

Beulah looked round and waited for Denise to take a seat first, then perched opposite on Sadie's old rocking chair.

'Is it alright to sit here?' She glanced

at Sadie's knitting bag at the side of the chair.

'Yeah, go ahead. Anyway, it's great to see you. It's surprising how long the day can be when all you're told to do is rest.'

'I know, it sounds like a dream situation to me, but then again . . .' She looked at Denise's foot. 'Not if you're restricted with moving around. Bet you've read all the magazines in the house.'

'Tell me about it and watched my favourite DVDs — still, I can always watch them again. I'm just so disappointed about missing the start date of the job.'

'Yes, lucky you — I saw the advert, but it wouldn't be enough hours for me. I'm waiting until I hear back from that magazine — remember the one I was telling you about? They want an intern for the summer, on the fashion pages. All I have to do is read and study fashion mags, then write up a blog and do a few articles.'

'Sounds great.' Denise looked up as Sadie came in with a tea and toast for two. 'Oh, Sadie, that looks a treat.'

'Carry on talking — don't mind me, I'm off outside. Time I'd got those sweet pea seeds in.' Smiling at the pair, she left the room, taking her own mug of tea outside to the back garden.

'Anyway, enough about me, how's things with you? Are you still getting on well with Tony? He was trying to impress you, last time we spoke.'

Denise reached for another slice of toast, spread thickly with butter and marmalade. Nodding to the plate, she indicated for Beulah to help herself.

'Not for me, I've had two slices already, got to watch the . . . ' she tapped her middle, and gave Denise a wink.

'Oh, I see, getting closer and want to make sure you're in perfect shape.' Denise gave a cheeky giggle. 'What's the latest, then?'

Beulah leaned in closer towards her friend.

'He's got tickets for Ascot.' She sat back and her eyes sparkled like gems. 'Can you imagine? As if I've ever been to the races! I have always wanted to go . . . but Ascot!'

Picking up on her friend's enthusiasm, Denise gasped.

'Oh my word, what are you going to wear?' Her amber eyes flashed with hints of gold as she waited to hear.

'That's the thing, I've got this lovely plum coloured suit.' Beulah stood up and wiggled as she waved her hands down her sides. 'Fitted skirt comes to just below the knee. Little boxy kind of jacket, and I've got a pink frilly blouse to go under that. Black clutch bag, and then I wanted a really neat hat to go with it. Do you think I can find one?' She tutted and pulled a face.

'If I wanted a fascinator, there'd be hundreds to choose from, but can you imagine, really, me with a wisp on my head! I'm doing well to wear a skirt. To be honest, I'd have been more at home in a trouser suit, but you can't go to

Ascot and not dress up, can you? As for where they all get these elaborate hats — beats me.' Beulah sat back looking quite deflated.

Denise was scribbling on the pad left out from the day before. She looked up at her friend, closed her left eye slightly, and then tilted her head.

'Mm, a neat trilby style maybe, with a hint of feminine glamour in the way of ribbon. Then something to complement your eyes, like a peacock feather, or half of one at the side.'

All the time she sketched and tilted her head, keeping an eye on the oval shape of Beulah's face. 'Or we could go for one with a wide brim, which would keep the sun off your face. It can be hot and there's no escaping the sun at the races, I would imagine.' Finally Denise passed her sketch pad across with the two designs.

Beulah's eyes lit up.

'Yes! If only. Where can I buy it? Don't tell me they've got them in Something Special. They haven't, I popped in there the other day. They had lots of straw hats, but nothing a patch on those.' She nodded towards the page in front of her.

'Tell you what.' Denise's amber eyes flashed an even darker shade of gold. 'I'll make you one.'

'I really wish you could, honestly, Denise. I'd pay you to create something like that. The trilby one might look smart, and the other one looks more glam. I'd say the trilby is more me, wouldn't you?'

Denise was nodding.

'I'm going to have a go. If it works out well, you'll have a hat for Ascot. If it turns out rubbish, well, I was going to say, I could put it towards my craft project for college. I'll practise until I get it right and make you the hat of your dreams. You wait and see.'

Denise gave her friend a reassuring smile, wondering whether she'd really be able to keep her rash promise.

3

'I'll need to buy some felt and scraps of material from the market — or I could have a look online.' Denise was buzzing with thoughts of her new project.

Sadie washed her hands at the sink, and picked up the towel nearby to wipe them.

'It's a great idea to keep your mind active, and if you're only practising, there's an old trunk in the back bedroom.' She raised her eyes towards the ceiling. 'Leftover stock they let us take home when we were made redundant from the Hat Factory. I've never got round to doing anything with it. You're welcome to have a look through.'

She placed bacon under the grill, and began peeling mushrooms. 'Not saying as you'll need half the things in there, it's a bit of a mixed bag really. Or a mixed trunk, I should say.' She popped the mushrooms into the frying pan.

Denise waited until the following morning, after Sadie had gone to catch the bus at the end of the road. Her weekly visit to town would mean she'd be out for at least three hours. Denise never normally went into the small bedroom, but now she had permission to rummage.

She found the trunk in the corner. It looked old and dusty, like one of those travel types from Victorian times when citizens of the British Empire went around the world on huge liners.

Delving in, Denise knew she'd opened a treasure chest. Squares of felt in all colours were piled high, along with bunches of ribbons and lace. Peach and pink scrunched flowers, crochet squares, metallic buttons in all shapes and sizes. How had she never seen all this? She gaped in wonder at the materials she had to work with.

On the table in the living room, Denise laid out a piece of black felt.

Carefully placing the pattern pieces she'd cut earlier on top, she used tailor's chalk and pins from Sadie's sewing box to secure them. When she'd used up all the pins, tilting her head to one side, she chewed on her lower lip as she cut carefully round the pattern pieces.

Next she set up the iron, and began to steam and stretch the material with her fists. It moved surprisingly easily, and soon she had a piece of fabric that was much more pliable to work with, and an oval shape where Beulah's head would go. Utterly engrossed, she didn't hear Sadie come through the back door loaded with a shopping bag in each hand.

'You're hatting! That's not bad.' Sadie plonked herself on a chair and reached out to examine Denise's first efforts. 'Why didn't you say you were starting this today? I'd have reached my hat block out of the loft for you.' She shrugged her coat off. 'Hang on, I'll get the step ladder, and see if I can find it.'

Denise tutted and took the ladders from her landlady.

'I can't let you climb up into the loft on these. I've hurt my foot, not my entire body. I'll be careful; you hold the bottom to steady me.'

Slowly dragging the ladders upstairs, and along the landing, she placed them under the hatch to the loft. Denise took each step steadily, being sure to keep most of her weight on the left foot and feeling rather clumsy. She removed the loft hatch with a shove, sending a cloud of dust scattering her face. She spluttered.

'Tell me, what is it I'm looking for?'

'My hat block,' Sadie shouted up as she gripped the ladder firmly with both hands. 'You'll need this as well by the way.' She passed a small torch up into Denise's outstretched hand.

'I know it's a hat block, but what does it look like? I've never heard of one, never mind seen one.' She took a peep round the dingy loft, noticing the huge cobwebs dangling from the eaves

45

more than anything else.

'It resembles the shape of a head, but made of wood,' said Sadie, 'a fleshy colour.'

'I'll get up there and have a feel around.' Denise put her hands on the ledge of the loft and heaved herself, ungainly, into the black hole.

'Will you be careful? Don't fall through the ceiling, whatever you do.'

Denise popped her head back through the gap.

'I'll try my best not to.' She grinned and turned herself round slowly and laboriously.

'Ah, I think I can see it.' Denise shone the small torch that Sadie had handed to her. She crawled on her belly across the boards that covered the beams and which prevented her from falling through.

'This, you mean?' She slid back towards the opening and passed the oval item she'd found out to Sadie.

'That's the one! Now, you be careful coming down. I don't want you to fall.'

* * *

'Pass me the steam iron, and I'll show you what we did next.'

Denise watched her landlady pulling a fresh piece of brown felt over the block of wood.

'We had all the machines at the factory, of course. There was a room, oh,' Sadie looked out of the back window, 'it'd be as far as from here to the canal, and twice as wide. The steam would be billowing out and the clatter and clanging of the machines almost sent you deaf.'

Watching closely, Denise noticed how the shape of the hat was beginning to form. The steam iron gave the felt more firmness with much hissing and spluttering.

'We used shellac, but you could use diluted PVA glue — works just as well. Make sure it's watered down, though, otherwise it'll go lumpy. You'll need six parts water to one part glue if I remember rightly. You have a go — it's a matter of practice, and nobody ever got a hat right first time. Trust me.'

Sadie left her to it, and settled down in the other room to watch her favourite soap.

Denise cut the pattern out again, steaming first, shaping then steaming again. She applied her PVA mix with Sadie's pastry brush, making a mental note to buy her a new one when she next ventured into town.

'It's getting better,' she called, hopping clumsily next door to seek Sadie's approval.

'Keep on practising. I'll show you how to attach the brim tomorrow.'

Reluctant to abandon her work, Denise limped to the kitchen. It was her turn to make the nighttime drinks.

* * *

The following morning, seated back at the table, Denise searched online and found a hat-making workshop. She spent a whole hour studying before giving it another go.

'It's easier than I imagined it would be,' she shouted to Sadie.

'It can be as easy or tricky as you want to make it, really, depending on the design. You've already got a flair for sewing.'

Coming to sit by her side, Sadie watched as Denise used the measurements Beulah had given her.

'So that's Beulah's head — ' Denise drew the oval shape, taking note of the measurements. 'Now this part goes around the head to form the brim and needs to be at least three inches thick.' She checked that Sadie was in agreement.

'Allow for seams as well, don't forget.' Sadie raised her eyebrows.

'Of course.' Denise gave her a look that said, *I'm not totally stupid.*

'What if we wanted a stiffer brim, though?' Rubbing her hand across her lips, Denise frowned.

'You'd either use a stiffening fabric, or more of the PVA mix.' Sadie smiled and squeezed Denise's shoulder. 'Don't expect to get it perfect straight away, love. It took ages for us to train up in the factory, you know. Even then, some couldn't ever pick it up. They went to the packing department, or some stayed on cutting, or steaming. That's how it was. We all mucked in and worked together.'

'Must have been really hard work, though.' Denise studied the older lady, hoping to hear more of her days in the Hat Factory.

Sadie smiled.

'Oh, it was that, but we had plenty of laughs as well. We all looked forward to the jokes. Some would make your hair curl, even now and the boss there was so dishy you wouldn't believe.' She made an imaginary fan with her hand and wafted it in front of her face. 'Some would break the needle on their machine just so he'd come and check it out. Not me, of course.' She smiled devilishly.

'Ah, I didn't know you had a crush.'

'If you'd seen him . . . oh, talk about attractive. Everyone between twenty and ninety swooned over him. All this curly dark hair and those eyes, you've never seen anything like it I'll tell you.'

Sadie had gone all glassy-eyed and Denise knew she wouldn't have much more hat instruction now she was off on a daydream. The knock on the back door broke the spell.

'Only me . . . ' Joe popped his head round the door. 'I'll just kick my muddy boots off.' A few minutes later he was in the room and holding out a bunch of Sweet Williams.

'For the patient, recommended for a quick recovery.' He smiled. 'I picked them this morning, off the allotment. They're one of my favourites — thought you might like some.'

'They're gorgeous.' Denise took the flowers, burying her face in the purple and pink ripples of colour. 'Mmm, they smell divine.' She passed Joe a chair, and made her way to the kitchen. 'Like a cuppa, Joe? And how's your mum?'

'As long as it's not that flowery tea you two like to drink. I'm a gardener, remember. I'll have a cup of the strong stuff if you've got any. Mum's feeling brighter, thanks.'

Denise popped her head round the kitchen door. 'That's good news.'

'Aye, it was more of a shock than too much damage done. Little bit of bruising, she's got the witch hazel on hand for that. You know how she is with healing herself when she can?'

'That's good news.' Sadie nodded. 'I'm doing a hotpot for Sunday lunch — tell her we'll pop her some round.'

'That's a kind offer. I'm glad she's got you two next door. Takes a lot of worry off me and our Vera, knowing you're on hand for her. I dread to think what might have happened if you hadn't been next door, Sadie.' He looked kindly towards Sadie, who flapped her hand and shook her head.

'What are good neighbours for? She'd have done the same for me, I know.'

'I could say the same for you.' Denise laid the tea tray on the table and passed the mugs around. 'How you carried me along the canal the other day . . . anybody would think you were a weight lifter.' She smiled at Joe who chuckled.

'Tell you what, I'll pop along and give you a hand on the allotment.' She raised her plaster-covered foot. 'Whenever this dratted foot gets better. You've been so kind, I'd like to repay you.'

Denise wasn't a brilliant gardener, but she did intend to stick to her word.

★ ★ ★

The pile of felt was getting smaller. Now Sadie had a hat to wear in the garden, and Beulah's Ascot creation was taking shape, too. On her short walks down the garden to sit by the canal on her favourite bench, Denise had accumulated several types of feathers. A bluey-green one would be perfect on the black hat she'd formed for her friend.

It was while she was sitting there, watching a barge chug lazily past, and sketching more designs, that she heard Sadie calling her.

The familiar creak from the garden gate made her turn. Craig Spencer was walking towards her, pausing to watch the colourful barge drifting past. Denise froze for a second, and then heard Sadie call as she leaned over the gate.

'You've got a visitor, love.' She gave Denise a wave, and went back to her garden.

He took his eyes from the barge.

'Nothing like the smell of wood smoke along a canal, is there?' He sat down beside her and watched the barge disappear round a corner.

Denise could smell the freshness of soap that she guessed to be sandalwood. She hardly dared turn and look at him for fear of going a tomato shade of red. What did he want? If it were to tell her that she'd been replaced in the job, she couldn't bear the disappointment.

Turning to face him, she noticed those dark curls glinting in the afternoon sun. His tanned face was full of vitality and the white shirt was teamed with pale denim jeans, slightly worn at the knees.

Kingfisher-blue eyes looked straight into hers. When he spoke, that deep velvet voice made her shiver inside. Denise pulled her cardigan round her shoulders and tilted her head to listen.

4

'I fly out to Paris tomorrow.' His eyes followed a pair of swans as they floated past, close to the canal bank.

Denise found it impossible to stop her eyes straying to where his open-necked shirt revealed more dark curls . . . and those denim-clad thighs were slightly too close for her to be relaxed.

'For work reasons, is it?' She cleared her throat and put her sketches to one side.

Craig nodded. 'Fashion week. We get to see what's hot on the catwalk, and what's not.'

'Like those way-out dresses made of paperclips, and oversized men's suits, you mean?' As soon as the words had tumbled from her lips she wished she could dive into a hole in the ground. Why mock what he did for a living? What an idiot. She'd made herself sound like a jealous lover rather than a soon-to-be employee.

'I wouldn't expect to see anything like that.' He gave her a sideways glance, and then looked down to the plaster cast covering her foot. 'How's it feeling?'

Did he care, or was he just checking up? Like one of those visits when you've missed Sunday school and the teacher calls round to catch you playing in the garden. 'It's getting better, thanks — it shouldn't be long now until I'm back to normal. The hospital gave me a note for three weeks, and then I'm hoping to come in to the shop.'

She stole a glance to check whether he'd come here to tell her otherwise.

'I didn't mean to be so rude, about the fashions — they're so way-out, that's all. Tell me about the fashion show. Will you be on the front row with all the magazine editors?'

Anna Wintour sprang to mind and she felt a pang. He gave off such an overwhelming male essence, he could have any woman he wanted — and probably did.

Suddenly Denise needed to know more about his life, even knowing she'd never be close to him . . . apart from now, on her favourite bench.

'One day, maybe — but no, not the front row, my tickets are for half way back. I need to catch all the latest designs. Be the shop that's talked about in wine bars and coffee shops around the country.' Craig looked almost shy for a moment, and his dark lashes hid anything that she could have read in his eyes. He was quiet for a moment, then stretched his legs out in front of the bench and drew his arms to a folded position behind his head.

'My vision is to supply beautiful garments to ladies of all ages. In the Midlands first, then country-wide. After that, who knows?' He turned to face Denise. From the look on his face, she knew he meant every word.

He glanced over her clothes and she wished she were wearing something more flattering than her comfortable, faded T-shirt and the patchwork skirt she'd designed and made herself, topped off with her old baggy cardigan. If he'd called to say he was popping by, she could have made more of an effort.

'Everyone heads for Stratford and Warwick . . . why not Mullsey?' He pulled at a tuft of grass from by the bench, and threw it towards the water. 'This area was famed for manufacturing, wasn't it? There was the shoe factory, knitwear, a couple or three hat factories. It's time to get Mullsey back on the map.'

He smiled, and laughter lines by his eyes made him even more attractive — if that were possible.

'We'll be the ones providing unique fashions. People will always go for quality if it's something special, at Something Special.'

He raised an eyebrow and leaned closer, eyes sparkling. His warm smile caused her insides to lurch.

'I'm looking forward to getting back

and going over the new collections with the team. You'd be welcome to join us and take a look if you'd like.'

His vibrant blue eyes held hers, and Denise wondered how a woodpecker had moved into the place her heart normally was.

Trying to control her breathing that was becoming slightly heavier, she swallowed. Not trusting herself to speak, she nodded and smiled. Maybe if she placed her hand on his thigh and risked missing out on the job, it would be worth it . . . She restrained herself and instead gathered her things.

'That would be lovely. Is it getting cool out here, or is it me?' she mumbled. In reality she was feeling flustered and needed to get into the house, safely away from the sight and scent of the man by her side. She didn't trust her actions, and she'd only been near him twice!

'Well, that's all I came to say — and to check you were alright, of course.'

The sound of his voice sent her

reeling again. No man had ever had this effect on her before. Her few past relationships had turned out so badly, she'd given up. Her last partner had said, 'Wait for me . . . I want to travel and see the world. I'll be back for you when I've lived my life.' She'd told him to go and find a life without her in it.

Glad to hear that her new employer was completely focused on his business plan and making a go of it, Denise forced all thoughts of boyfriends and attractive men like the gorgeous Craig Spencer completely out of her mind.

He took her arm and helped her through the squeaky gate, up the pathway to the cottage. After the initial electrifying thrill, his touch made Denise feel secure. His body was gym-toned, and he clearly took care of himself. There was nothing about him that she didn't like. Except for the inconvenient fact that her insides turned to mush whenever he was near.

Feeling more confident once she was

back inside, she explained to Sadie who Craig was.

'I know, love, we had a chat earlier.'

If Denise wasn't mistaken, Sadie had more of a twinkle in her eye than usual and was that lipstick she'd applied? As she'd already worked out, no woman could be immune to the charms of the handsome Mr Spencer.

'And I'm still trying to think of that actor we watched on television last night. He looked the spit of you — now, what was that good-looking man called, Denise? You remember the one.'

For heaven's sake, what was Sadie thinking?

'No, I can't remember who you mean, Sadie. I wasn't watching television with you anyway.' Irritated by the way she was being dragged into some debate about good-looking actors and comparing them to the man she was hoping to work for was not something Denise was interested in. Whether he noticed her unease, she couldn't tell.

'I brought some brochures, a hint of

what might be on show in Paris. I thought you'd like to have a browse.' A devilish grin played around his lips. 'Not a paperclip in sight. We'll chat when I come back.'

Both Sadie and Denise were captivated by the man with the dark curls and the cute smile. Craig himself seemed oblivious to the effect he was having on both of them.

'Talk soon.' He gave a hint of a wink, and left Denise feeling a warm glow all over. She watched from the front window as his dark blue E-Type Jaguar revved into gear and disappeared up the road with the same panache as its owner.

'Well, now I see why you're eager to start work.' Sadie gave an exaggerated nod towards the door. 'He actually makes my old boss at the hat factory seem rather feeble. No, tell a lie — he could be related with those looks.'

'Hold it right there. I'm looking forward to working with the dresses, getting to know more about fashion.'

Denise pulled at her patchwork skirt. 'Heavens, let's face it, I'd never have worn this old skirt if I'd known he was going to turn up.' She raised her eyes to the ceiling and tutted.

'My point exactly, you're bothered what he thinks, that's always a sign.' Sadie beamed.

'Stop presuming. He's polite, funny and, alright, I'll admit he's not the ugliest man I've ever met, but definitely not my type. I couldn't handle a man like that.'

Turning so that Sadie couldn't see the heat colouring her cheeks, Denise left the room. She'd had enough excitement for one day and an argument with Sadie wasn't on her list of things to do . . . especially knowing she was not a million miles from the truth.

★ ★ ★

'If you carry on making good progress, we'll take the plaster off in a couple of weeks.' Dr Malik took notes as Denise carefully rotated her ankle. 'You've been walking on it as well, you said?'

'Around the house, and short walks,' she told him. 'Mostly I'm resting it and keeping it up. I really will be glad to get back to normal, though.' She gave a half-smile. 'It's nice to have time for doing things I've always wanted to do, but there's only so much . . .'

'Well, that's the second plaster cast now — it's only a matter of using it a bit more, and seeing your own doctor until we can fix a date for you to come back and have it removed.'

He ticked boxes on his sheet and giving a satisfied nod to the duty nurse, moved on with his rounds.

Taking the bus back from Mullsey General, Denise stopped off in town rather than going straight home. It had been a while since she'd been out. There were a few toiletries on her list and she couldn't keep asking Sadie to shop for her all the time. A new blouse, ready for when she started work, was another thing she must get.

That was what prompted her to show her face in Something Special rather than waiting until the day she could walk in there properly without these dratted crutches getting in the way.

A quick glimpse through the window indicated to Denise that it wasn't Maud behind the counter. She'd spoken to Linda on the phone, and there was Jeanie who she hadn't met yet — it would be one or other of them.

She pushed herself against the door with her back facing the glass, and swung round to enter. Her ungainly entrance caused the woman to walk round from behind the counter.

'Can you manage? It can't be easy having to get around like that.' She glanced to where Denise had rested her still-swollen foot.

'I was passing, and called in to say hi.' She forced a smile. 'Obviously I'd rather not be stuck with this.' She raised her foot. 'A silly mistake for a moment, and now I've to wait another two weeks before it comes off.'

'You must be Denise. I'm Linda. Of course, I recognise your voice, we spoke on the phone when you first had the accident didn't we?' Her smile was as warm as the cockney lilt in her voice. 'I've heard all about you, and before you ask, all good. Maud thinks you'll fit in great. We're all down-to-earth. Maud sometimes puts on a bit of a voice.' She giggled. 'No use in me trying anything like that now, is there? I'm from London, as you might have twigged.' She gathered a pile of hair accessories from the counter and turned to a nearby stand. 'We've had these new in this morning; with the better weather forecast he's expecting everyone to be tying their hair up. Not me, I like my flicks.' She patted her immaculately styled blonde hair and filled up the stand.

'You've moved here recently, then?' Denise enquired.

'No, been around the Midlands for years. My hubby, Ronnie, works on the roads. He came down south, and then when he found there was going to be more jobs in Nottingham, I moved with him. That was over twenty years ago. We only recently moved here, though. Craig asked me if I wanted to be the assistant buyer when he opened the shop.'

'Oh, wow! That's exciting. You knew him before, obviously.'

'He had market stalls in Nottingham, started off in ladies' tights.' Linda chuckled and gave Denise a nudge. 'You'll never know how much teasing he's had for that over the years. He's a great bloke, though — there's nothing about women's fashion he doesn't know.' She nodded to Denise who realised there was quite a lot about Craig Spencer she had yet to discover.

While they were talking, the door pinged, and a couple of ladies entered and marched over to the silk blouses that were hanging next to trousers in colours to match.

'I've got my eye on this one.' One of them held up a cream blouse with dark chocolate squares all over.

'These would go well with that, Elsa.' They busied themselves mixing and matching until they asked Linda if they could try them on.

'By all means, you know where to go . . . ' She pulled a velvet curtain across to reveal a cubicle. 'There's another one at the back of the shop if you both need one.'

Turning to Denise, she put a hand on her arm.

'Oh, where are my manners? Like a cuppa? We've always got the kettle on, and I fancy a brew.'

Without waiting for a reply, Linda stepped into the kitchen, turning back to talk at the same time.

'Will this be your first job. then, Denise?'

Her questions were friendly without being nosey, and as she answered, Denise sensed she'd get on well with Linda. She felt lighter inside now she'd met another of the ladies in Craig's team.

'Maud made me feel welcome, and you have as well,' she explained. She began to feel excited at the thought of being among these lively ladies. 'There's only Jeanie I haven't met now.'

Denise paused in the hope that Linda might tell her about the remaining shop assistant.

'Jeanie is hot . . . ' Linda passed a mug across to Denise. 'Like this tea — be careful with it. I've used powdered milk, so it's scalding.'

'She's a model?' Denise remembered Craig telling her about checking out who was hot and who was not on the catwalk.

'Cripes, not a model — though she could be. I meant hot as in selling all this.' She gave a nod towards the clothing. 'She'll think nothing of jump-ing in her car and going out on the knocker . . . sorry, love, you'll get used to me. She'll go around and find business if there's a slack period. That's why Craig wanted her to come over here. She'll stand in the shop well enough, and she's great with the customers; speaking of which, excuse me a mo'.'

She left Denise wondering about Jeanie and how Craig seemed to like things hot, and then a vision of him in tights made her smile. Finishing her drink, she looked to where Linda was telling the older lady, who'd emerged from the cubicle, that she looked wonderfully elegant in the outfit.

She manoeuvred her crutches and hauled herself to her feet.

'I'll be back in two weeks — so glad I came in. Thanks for the drink; it was good to meet you.'

As Denise pulled the shop door open, Linda ran after her.

'Hey, listen, we'll get on like a house on fire, and it's not all feather boas and silky knickers in here, you know. Now, excuse me, we may have a sale. See you soon, me old china.'

Denise made her way towards the bus station with a smile on her face, thankful that the stop was only metres from where they lived.

* * *

'Sadie, you'll never know how great that feels.' Wiggling her toes as she lifted them out of the foot spa, Denise planted her feet firmly on the waiting towel. 'The bruising has almost gone now, look. Thank goodness for our Health Service. They've been brilliant. I'd never moan. Those nurses are angels, and Dr Malik said it might take four to five weeks, so he knows what he's on about.'

'That's what I always say. We hear some shocking stories on the news, but in real life, when we need them, they're always there. So far anyway — touch wood.' Sadie looked round and tapped her fingers on the sideboard. 'I'm really pleased with my new gardening hat, thank you.' She reached towards the basic peasant-style hat with the floppy brim, keeping the teapot warm. 'Oh, cosy!' She pulled it firmly down.

'It's shabby chic, boho style. On trend, as the celebs would say.' Denise was pulling her leg. She often referred to her own dress style as boho and shabby chic if she'd picked something up in the second hand shop. 'It'll keep the sun off, and keep you warm if there's a breeze.'

'How have I managed without one until now?' Sadie pulled a face of mock horror. 'No, seriously, love, you've done really well. I'm proud of you. You could have been bored out of your mind, but the time's been well spent when you've got this to show for it. How's Beulah's trilby coming along, anyway?'

'Almost done — and look what I found by the second oak tree along the canal yesterday. I forgot to tell you.' Denise pulled a cluster of feathers from the box near where she sat.

'Let's see.' Putting her glasses on, Sadie leaned forward to inspect the feathers. 'Looks like a mallard to me. Either got caught by a fox, or a cat maybe. Were there many feathers there?'

'No, only these.' Denise held the treasures carefully. 'I'd hate to think of a lovely little duck getting hurt, but there wasn't any sign of a fight.'

'More than likely it's been moulting, then, or grooming itself. Don't worry too much — if the feathers were abandoned, you're hardly plucking it bald, are you? Teddy would help you out with things like that, though.' Sadie took her specs off and leaned back on her rocker.

'Who's Teddy? Oh . . . the old game-keeper.' Denise wrapped the feathers in tissue paper and put them away.

'He's always got supplies for the local fly fishermen. Why not pay him a visit when you feel up to it?'

'I may just do that. I'll text Beulah and tell her she'll be able to have a look at the hat soon.'

★ ★ ★

'These are the new lines.' Carefully Maud handed Denise a pile of dresses, similar in style but different colours. 'Don't you just love the madness of Marc Jacobs? These floaty and baggier designs could have been made for me.'

She held layers of an orange and pale peach midi dress against her robust shape and sashayed towards the mirror. The dress was shaped like nothing Denise had seen before, except maybe one of her own creations that had gone wrong. Then she thought how all those times she could have been a dress designer, and those unique items she'd thrown away might not have been that bad after all.

'They're adorable,' she said mistily, wondering if she'd get chance to try one on.

'You approve of my selections?' Denise hadn't heard Craig come up behind them as they were looking at the new range. 'And we have several black and white classics for those less adventurous types.' He flicked a glance at Denise and immediately she picked up the most colourful garment from the pile.

'What's the point of black and white when things like this are on offer?' She held up a peasant-style blouse with colourful birds and leaves embroidered across the top. 'Imagine this with a pair of those new flared trousers, in vibrant blue.' She suddenly became aware of those eyes that seemed to invite her somewhere she wasn't sure she was ready to go. 'Or a bright sunflower yellow or . . . ' She was glad when Maud interrupted her ramblings.

'Takes me back to the Seventies! We had the original flares. These seem more glamorous somehow, though.' She admired the range of baggy, hot-from-the-catwalk trousers. 'Yes, great choices, Craig, you've selected the best clothes I've seen in a long while. Any woman, whatever her age, would look special wearing anything from this range. You've got a good eye, I'll say that.'

'Steady on, Maud. You'll be getting

your platforms out next.' Craig laughed. 'I'll get the kettle on. Tea, everyone?' He disappeared into the kitchen.

* * *

The morning went by so quickly that Denise almost forgot that Beulah had said she'd call in to see how the hat experiment was coming on. Only when the door pinged and her friend walked into the shop, did she remember.

'Oh, hi! Hang on a minute, I'll get my phone, it's in my bag.'

Making her way to the kitchen, Denise put the kettle on in readiness for the afternoon tea break. She knew Craig would be down soon as it was the ritual she'd come to recognise each Saturday since she'd started.

One of the main things she liked about Craig Spencer — apart from his blue eyes, dark hair and tanned face, together with the way his jeans fitted perfectly around his behind — was the sound of his voice, but the absolute main thing she liked about her new boss was the relaxed atmosphere he'd created in the shop. He encouraged chatter and often came down and mingled with customers. Almost casual, yet he had a way of gaining respect without demanding it. The team of ladies he had were all on friendly terms with him, and Denise was glad she'd made the decision to call and ask for the job a few weeks ago.

She showed Beulah the picture of the black trilby with the mallard's feather she'd found by the canal. Maud and Linda had told her that as long as she wasn't continuously on her phone, it was alright to use it if need be.

She highlighted the best shot of the black trilby, and the turquoise feather with a touch of burgundy did look almost professional, Denise thought.

'I love it!' Beulah swung round and zoomed in on the picture to have a closer look. 'Is that it finished? Denise, that feather matches the colour of the suit in parts. It's got a lovely sheen to it. Is it a peacock feather?'

By now Craig had heard the chatter and was in the shop, looking interested.

'Look what my clever friend has made for me.' Beulah was more excited than Denise thought she would be.

'You haven't seen the real object yet,' Denise said, pulling the original sketches from her pocket. 'It's meant to be like this.'

'Let me see.' Craig frowned and moved in closer.

As Denise handed him the paper with those first scribbles she'd sat and designed in Sadie's front room, Craig moved in swiftly.

'Do you mind?' He whipped his mobile from the back pocket of his chinos, and took a picture of the art work. 'I'd really like you to send me that finished one as well.' His eyes gleamed.

'It's only a hat she wanted for Ascot.' Denise blushed and wished she'd kept it quiet.

'No, it's fabulous. When can I see it? Are you home tonight?' Beulah handed the phone back to Denise, and glanced at her watch. 'I'll pop back another time and try something on.' She stroked an all-in-one catsuit in shimmering gold. 'That's funky. See you later on.'

When she'd gone, and Craig had retreated upstairs, Maud tidied up the scarves.

A niggling feeling was itching away in the back of Denise's mind. Why had Craig wanted to take pictures of her designs? She hoped he wasn't one of those men who would be showing people and having a laugh at her expense later on. From now on, she'd keep her hobby to herself.

5

'Seriously, you've worked wonders. It's amazing. How much do I owe you?' Beulah twirled around in Sadie's front room and looked first left then right at her reflection in the mirror.

'I've come in the whole outfit so you can see how the colours look together, and then tell me if it works.' She glanced at Denise. 'Or whether I'll need to look for something else. This outfit isn't concrete.'

'It's too soft for that.' Denise leaned over and rubbed the hem of the fabric between her fingers. 'Owe me? Go away . . . I'm glad to have the practice. If you hadn't told me you wanted a special hat, I wouldn't have dreamed of having a go at being a milliner and luckily for me, there was a professional hatter on hand to assist. It helped fill my days and gave me something to occupy my mind while resting my foot.'

Only for a second, an image of a man with laughing blue eyes wearing an open-necked shirt drifted across her consciousness. She pushed it to the back of her mind, and turned towards where her friend was still looking in the mirror.

'I wouldn't have believed how involved hat making could be — and fairly easy, after a lot of mishaps.'

'Mis-hats, you mean?' Beulah grinned. 'No, I love it and you know what I mean when I say not concrete. This isn't my fixed outfit, but top of the list. Unless I go for that gold catsuit I spotted the other day in Something Special! This feels comfortable, though — and quite dressy, for me, don't you think?' Beulah tugged at the short jacket and fiddled with the lapels.

'If Tony could see you he'd be wolf whistling.' Denise stood back in admiration. 'He might even think of making you Mrs Bradley. Then again, you'd be the one doing any proposing with that smart 'I'm in charge' look you've got going on. Come here.'

She grabbed her phone and took several pictures of her friend in her new outfit, topped off with the trilby, complete with mallard feather and black velvet bow. Beulah, caught up in the moment, struck a Bond girl pose, hand on hip with cat walk swivel, moody pout included.

'We need to go somewhere — give you chance to show off that great new look, and I'm coming with you. I'll go and have a quick shower.' Before Beulah had chance to reply, Denise was half way up the stairs. 'Even though I'll look like your older sister — you do glam like nobody else I know,' she shouted back down through the banisters.

Digging deep into her wardrobe she searched for something that might not look out of place with her friend's trendy outfit.

She selected a pale blue fitted dress with diagonal stripes of a darker blue.

Not exactly riveting, but with the dark pink belt she kept dangling on the bed post, fastened round the middle, it made a smart enough outfit, she thought. She selected pale blue wedges to wear over her skin tone tights. Quickly showering and changing, she grabbed her make-up bag and applied mascara and lipstick in a colour to match the belt. Pulling her hairbrush through her golden locks, she was good to go. She topped off her look with a box-style navy jacket.

'That was a quick transformation. Where did you fancy going? Mullsey town?'

Denise drew back a step. 'No, I thought we'd take the train into Birmingham. The station has changed since I last went and the Centenary Square will be a great open space to show off your new look, judging by the weather. I'll just stick my head in next door, let Sadie know we're going, and tell her not to bother with anything to eat for me. We can grab some pizza in an Italian bar.'

Beulah nodded eagerly. 'Yes, we'll drink wine and have a good old gossip.'

At the end of the road they caught the bus into Mullsey, and from the station, took the direct train to Birmingham New Street. They chatted during the entire journey, and almost missed their stop.

Beulah constantly placed her hand to the side of her head.

'Just checking,' she said. 'I don't very often wear a hat. It feels secure really — it does.' She held her head high and Denise felt a shiver of pride when she thought of those six or seven failed attempts; now her friend looked every inch the lady, ready for Ascot in her trilby.

'We could pop and see the library,' Beulah suggested. 'I still haven't been in there and it's massive. There are some fashion books I could flick through. We've got all afternoon, haven't we?'

'Yeah, and I want to look round the

rag market and have a rummage afterwards. I can have a look at the latest fashion magazines with you as well while we're in the library. Do a bit of homework as well as a day out for us.' Denise looked out of the window and watched the fields and farmland whizzing by.

'No wonder you wanted to come to the city then — nothing to do with showing off my get-up.' Beulah laughed. 'Of course we'll go there first. I'd love to come with you. This is the start of your new hatting empire — and all because of me, don't forget.'

'I'm sure you won't let me forget.' Denise smiled, glad to have the friendship of Beulah.

★ ★ ★

The dark blue E-Type Jaguar purred along Mullsey High Street, slowing down outside Something Special while the owner cast a critical eye over the frontage. He'd left instructions for

Denise to have a go at the window display this week.

Every second Friday evening, the display was changed ready for the weekend shoppers. With the change in the weather, those fruit and pastel floaty dresses would be sure to bring customers in on this fine Saturday morning in May.

Pleased with the bright colours she'd used and the addition of straw hats and sunglasses to the mannequins, Craig drove a few hundred yards past the shops and swung into Church Walk, then looped round to park in his usual space at the back of the shop.

As he locked the car, he thought of his grandma, who'd made his dream of owning an E-Type Jag possible. She'd died following a stroke, almost a year ago now. Thankfully she didn't suffer, and it came as a shock to find out she'd left her farmhouse cottage on the Welsh borders to him.

Craig thought of her often, and the little Welsh village where he'd spent summer holidays when he was growing up. His mother always told him he took after her side of the family with his dark hair and impulsive nature. That's why they hadn't been surprised when he'd promptly sold the cottage and used the money to buy his dream car — and to start up the business he'd been working towards since his schooldays.

He went through the usual morning routine of making coffee and checking the staff rota to see who was working alongside Denise today. It was Maud, so there was no need for him to linger for introductions. She'd yet to meet Jeanie, and he'd have made the time to be on hand if it was their first day together.

Pleased with the way his Saturday girl was turning out, Craig made his way upstairs to his office. Booting the laptop into action, he turned to open the small top window. He loved to keep fresh air circulating through the building, and the scents they used downstairs to keep the place smelling fresh sometimes overpowered him, though the customers seemed to love the jasmine and rose plug-in air fresheners that Maud insisted on placing in the sockets.

He heard the jangle of the front door unlocking and then chatter and laughter downstairs, followed by . . .

'Maud and Denise are now in the building, just so as you know.' A loud trill from the older lady drifted up the stairs.

'Okie-dokie.'

He'd go down after checking emails and dealing with any other business that needed attention. The fashion show had given him chance to broaden his horizons and go even bolder with plans for his latest collections. His new internet shop front, using the actual window of Something Special, was attracting customers from the surrounding counties, who were calling in person.

He studied an email from a new dress designer in Essex. He'd agreed to meet her, and now she was confirming that she'd be over during the following week as arranged, to show him her afternoon cocktail range.

Rubbing his hand across the back of his neck, Craig suddenly felt tired. He couldn't remember the last time a woman had placed cool hands across his aching shoulders. That side of his life had ground to a complete halt after the terrible matchmaking efforts of his so-called mates.

His parents were also too fond of asking, 'Have you met The One yet?'

If he had, they'd only get to know when he was a hundred percent sure himself.

Glancing at the old station clock, the one from his grandma's kitchen, he thought that now would be as good a time as any to go downstairs and mention to Denise that she'd done a tidy job with the window. He found her busy, still adding bracelets with matching necklaces to her display. Oversized handbags in colours to match the outfits were being strategically placed near the front of the window.

'Watch you don't fall back — it's easy when you're leaning across like that. I'm happy with the display. You have hidden talents, Miss Gambon.'

He could see in more detail, close up, how she'd used blocks of the same colour to give a more dramatic splash than last week's display.

'I'd like us to try and clear some of those handbags over the next few weeks if we can.' He swung around to Maud. 'I know I can count on you to talk them out of the door.' With a glance at Denise, he smiled. 'There's nothing she doesn't know about selling. She'll teach you more than you'd ever learn at college.'

'Don't you worry!' Maud informed him. 'She's already sold a few of those pastel jackets.'

Denise wished they'd stop talking about her as if she weren't there, or as if she was six years old. She nodded.

'Sadie told me she might call in

today. I told her about these Martinique kaftans.'

Arranging the folds of a calf-length orchid design, in light aubergine, Denise instinctively knew they'd be a hit with buyers. She glanced up.

'One of these would be even more comfortable than trackie bottoms. I could see her in one of these, either in the garden late afternoon, or in the evenings.' She was talking to Maud, and then she noticed Craig was still listening.

'Ah, now I understand why you've put them in the window. Smart move.' He gave Denise one of his warmest smiles.

He lives for his business. That's the only thing that makes him tick.

She supposed that his future wife, if he ever took time off from work to find one, would have to be someone in the fashion industry or a designer, engrossed in the trade just as he was.

Dusting herself down as she stepped out from the window, Denise moved to the opposite side of the shop and began placing newly arrived spring jackets onto an empty rail in order of size. Anything to get away from the gaze of the man with the sexiest, kindest eyes she'd ever seen.

★ ★ ★

'We'll have an iced bun with our afternoon drink,' Maud said and reached for her purse. 'My treat — you paid last week, didn't you?'

She handed Denise a five-pound note, and reminded her not to forget one for Craig.

'You'd think he'd be fat with the way he eats cake, wouldn't you?' Maud laughed.

'Some people can eat anything without it making any difference.' Denise pushed the note into her back pocket and made for the door.

'He goes to the gym most mornings. You don't get a body like that from sitting behind a desk on a computer all day. His mum's always telling me, she wonders when he's going to meet the right one and settle down. There can't be many women who wouldn't like to keep him warm at night — but to us he's just Craig, isn't he? We're lucky to work for an easy-going man like him. He'd do anything for us if we were stuck, you know. Kind-hearted as anything.'

It was at that moment the man in question chose to appear from upstairs. Denise wondered how much of the conversation he'd overheard, and felt glad she hadn't added anything to Maud's observations about him being fit and them being lucky to be working for him. She nipped out to get cakes before he had chance to speak.

There wasn't a queue in The Olde Tudor Bakery, and as Denise picked up her buns she turned and bumped into Sadie who had just walked in.

'I'm coming across to your place next. Thought we'd have pasties for tea — and salad, got to watch the waistline.

My skirt feels a bit tight.'

'Sounds yummy. Must dash, they're waiting for these.' She waved the iced buns above her head. 'Oh, and have a good look in the window before you come inside — there's something there that I think would really suit you.'

Minutes after Denise had returned, Sadie wandered into Something Special.

'Well, long time no see, Maud! So you're working here now. Denise has been telling me how you're helping her settle in.' Sadie gave her former work colleague a hug. 'I remember when you were the new girl, way back then.'

They exchanged affectionate smiles.

Denise was busy helping a young lady choose a dress for her engagement party from several gowns that were on offer. She acknowledged Sadie with a wink, and continued to give the customer her full attention.

Maud laughed.

'I'll never forget that first day. I was

terrified. You put me right, though, didn't you?'

'Of course I did and we had some laughs, didn't we?' Sadie began to recall some of the jokes, and then put her hand over her mouth. 'Don't think this is the place for the best ones, is it?'

Five minutes later, the engagement party customer was trying on a purple gown in the fitting room, and Denise was holding up the kaftan for Sadie, showing her the dark pink shade.

'This one will go better with your hair colour, and brings out the pink of your cheeks.'

'I'll try it on first, before I decide. Would it be alright to leave these somewhere? I wouldn't want anyone to trip over them.' Sadie looked down at her two bags of groceries.

'I'll keep them in the kitchen.' Maud took care of the shopping bags, while Denise pulled the curtain across the other changing room for Sadie.

'Psst! Is it alright to come in?' Beulah stuck her head through the doorway.

'It's always alright — we're a shop, you ninny.' Denise glanced over to where the ladies trying on were likely to emerge at any minute.

'I'm still wearing it! This hat's so comfy, I never want to take it off.' She patted her trilby and did a twirl. 'What do you think, Maud?'

'That's the one Denise made?'

Maud wasn't the quietest of ladies and her screams of admiration drifted upstairs to where Craig was sitting, weary of looking at the screen and updating his website.

The beeping sound from the till rang out across the shop floor as the purple gown was wrapped, bagged and sent out with another happy customer. Another beep followed with Sadie convinced she might need one of the large bags to go with the kaftan, for when she went on her next coach trip. Never mind relaxing in the garden — she wanted to get out and about to show it off.

'I'll be back,' Sadie declared, then

turned and noticing Craig, broke into a delighted smile. 'Now, Maud, you tell me. Does your boss remind you of anyone? Think back to our Hat Factory days.'

Denise cringed, and turned to where Beulah was flicking through a row of stylish jumpsuits.

'You do realise, if you change the outfit, it'll mean me making another hat?'

Craig ignored the who-does-he-remind-you-of question. He often got teased for looking like someone, and wished people would see beyond his appearance. He didn't regard himself as good-looking and found such comments an annoyance. He was far more interested in the trilby worn by the girl who was deep in conversation with Denise.

'That's the hat from the sketch? The one you had on your phone?'

He glanced at Beulah, and then carefully studied Denise's handmade craftwork.

'This is what my super-talented friend made for me, yes.' She did another twirl for added effect.

Craig nodded. 'Really beautiful, and clever as well.' He smiled slowly at Denise and gave an appreciative nod. 'And there was me thinking the Mullsey hat industry was finished.' He walked towards the back door. 'Lock up for me later if you could, please, Maud? I'm expected back in Lincoln-shire — a family gathering for Sunday lunch.' He only faintly raised his eyes towards the ceiling. 'Have a great rest of the weekend, all. See you next week.'

He'd already lifted the bulk of the day's takings, and trusted Maud to place any remaining cash in the safe behind the door in his office.

He knew he'd been right to employ his Saturday girl. Her talent was glaringly obvious. Maybe he could help her develop those skills — yet the thought of not seeing those amber eyes with flecks of gold every week filled him

with an emptiness he didn't want to
contemplate.

6

'We didn't mean to drop it on you at such short notice,' Jeanie was telling Denise. 'If you could work today, we'd be really grateful . . . Only Craig has been held up in Lincolnshire, and Maud rang in sick with a tummy bug. Must have been something she ate over the weekend, she thinks. So we were wondering if you would be able to help us out?'

Her college work was almost complete, and there wasn't anything vital that she couldn't catch up with at home. Denise made a snap decision, agreeing to cover for Maud.

'OK. I'll see you in a while, Jeanie. Looking forward to meeting you.'

Sadie pulled her small saucepan out from the cupboard under the sink.

'I was making beans on toast to keep you going. Will you still have time? I don't like to think of you only having cereal when you'll be on your feet for most of the day. You didn't have to say yes to them, love.'

'I've already told her I'll go in. Stop fussing, Sadie.'

'They could always close the shop, you know — or ask one of the others. You have to think of your college course.'

Denise immediately felt sorry she'd snapped.

'I know you mean well — you're just looking after me, I know that — but it's only for today, and I'll be finished at college soon. If they like how I'm fitting in at the shop, it might lead to extra days. Not as if anything was planned for today anyway.'

She gathered up her phone and scrolled down to the number for the college. After the receptionist connected Denise to her tutor, the woman said she was glad to have been informed, and told her it was alright.

Sadie shrugged and busied herself

preparing the hot breakfast.

'They shouldn't take advantage, that's all.'

Denise smiled, letting Sadie have the last word. There would be time for breakfast — especially one made with so much love.

★   ★   ★

If Denise had expected Jeanie to be anything like Linda or Maud, she couldn't have been more wrong. When she walked in, a slender woman with dark hair spiked onto her face, pixie-style, was behind the counter. She looked up when the doorbell tinkled, to reveal huge almond-shaped dark eyes.

'You're Denise?'

'Hello — Jeanie. It's me, yes.' Denise stood for a moment, not sure whether to shake hands with the woman or not. Most of the times she'd been in the shop up until now, Craig had either been upstairs or somewhere around. It felt a bit like her first day all over again.

The woman glanced back to the diary as if that were far more important.

'Glad you made it. Thing is, even though you're officially the Saturday girl, it makes it easier all round if you can be available to cover if we need you.' She fixed Denise with her dark brown eyes, seeming to be telling rather than asking.

'It's no bother today, only Craig said . . .'

'He's not here now, and I'm in charge whenever he's away. You may have settled in with the Golden Girls, but don't expect me to carry you. We are a team — don't get me wrong.'

Jeanie's olive skin glowed and her sculpted cheekbones appeared more angular now. She turned to pull the cord that lifted a blind covering the rear window, then swung back round. Her dark eyes were cold as she spoke. 'It's always left to me to keep things on track.'

Denise swallowed hard and the

muscles in the back of her neck grew tense. They'd all told her how they were one big happy team. This woman hadn't put her at ease at all, considering they'd only just met — and then she said something that felt like a smack in the stomach.

'He isn't available, you know.' Jeanie's eyes never left Denise for a second. 'In case you had any ideas in his direction.'

Then she smiled, but the venom in her words had paralysed Denise's heart.

It wasn't the welcome she'd been expecting for her first meeting with the third member of Craig's team. This one was more of a lone she-wolf.

When she'd spoken to Jeanie earlier and agreed to cover for Maud, the last thing she expected to find when she got here was someone warning her off from fancying the boss. As if!

'What? Me, have ideas . . . ? You think I'd . . . ' she gasped. 'That wouldn't enter my mind. This is Craig you're talking about, I presume?'

She did well to control the shaking, which was more from anger than fear. She gulped and coughed, hoping she'd be able to get through the next five minutes with this demon woman who seemed determined to make her feel small.

Even if she did have a slight mini crush on the man in question, she'd never let on to anyone — least of all Jeanie.

'Look . . . ' Stumbling over her words, she frowned, wanting to put things straight. The only alternative was to walk back through the door and never come back. She couldn't do that. 'I'm not sure what you're hinting at, but I've only been here a few weeks. Maud and Linda said . . . '

At the mention of the other team members, Jeanie let out a slow sigh. 'Yes, they're lovely, and Craig's lovely and we're a great little set-up. And I've had a bit of a night of it, to be honest. How are you at making strong black coffee?' She put down the pen in her hand and closed her eyes.

'Is something wrong?'

Knowing it would have been easier to escape to the kitchen and make the coffee, Denise didn't want to give the impression she had something to hide. How dare this complete stranger hint at her having designs on their boss?

'You and Craig, I didn't realise . . . Nobody told me, and I'm here for the work, not looking for a *man*.' She said the word with emphasis. She stood her ground and matched the stare of Ms Almond Eyes

'We're not a couple — good grief, not at all. You must be joking.'

The lady doth protest too much, methinks . . .

'Oh — from the way you were warning me off, it sounded as if . . . '

She was now curious as to why she'd been warned off Craig if this woman wasn't even his girlfriend.

'We're old friends — the type that watch out for each other. He's a good-looking guy and it gets him into trouble.' Jeanie raised her eyes towards the ceiling. 'Is there any chance of you getting that kettle on — please?' She indicated towards the kitchen and smiled properly for the first time that morning.

Seeing how the defensive look had left her eyes, Denise knew Jeanie wasn't totally the evil witch she'd made herself out to be. Though of all the team members, she was clearly the one to be most wary of. However Jeanie would learn that she wasn't just a little Saturday girl to be pushed around.

What kind of trouble did she mean? What had happened in Lincolnshire to prevent Craig from coming to work? Sometime over the course of the morning she hoped to find out.

'Someone, I can't remember who, told me you were the hot saleswoman,' she said.

She refused to be intimidated by the slender beauty of Jeanie. She flicked her blonde hair over her shoulder and waited for her to reply.

For a moment Jeanie looked at her as if she were a nuisance, and then smiled slowly.

'Really, I'm sure they have other names for me when I'm not around. Let's say if I've got fifty dresses to clear, I'll go out and make sure they're sold before I come back.'

Now Denise understood what kind of hot they were talking about.

'No wonder Craig wanted you to work with him, then.' She knew she was being cheeky, but there was nothing to lose. She needed to get to know what made Jeanie tick so that she could get along with her the same as she did with Linda and Maud.

They hadn't spelled out to her just how close Craig and Jeanie were, though. She wished they'd been a bit more upfront with her.

'We grew up together — more like brother and sister, you might say.'

Denise mixed coffee, listening attentively.

'You're originally from Lincolnshire, then?'

'That's where we're from, yes. Craig's mum originates from round here, though. She's friends with Maud — that's how she came to be working here. Linda and I helped Craig in his previous business. A drink would be lovely.'

Jeanie was smiling again, if a little woodenly, and Denise felt more at ease.

'Coming right up.' She poured the drinks and brought them through to the shop. 'What would you like me to do first?'

Denise so wanted to ask more questions, but decided not to push her luck, now she and Jeanie were on chatting terms.

'That's what I was coming round to next . . . you'll be alright to watch the shop by yourself, won't you? Don't think it'll be easy, but we wouldn't ask if we didn't think you were capable. Craig and I discussed it last night.'

Jeanie had that challenging look in her eye again, the one that made Denise feel obliged to say, 'Yes, of course I'll manage. Don't worry about a thing. I've been here long enough now.'

'I'm off to fetch Craig — he was delayed as I told you. He had a little problem with his car.' She muttered under her breath, 'Among other things.'

Trying to sound more confident than she actually felt, Denise said, 'Absolutely fine. I'll sell as if it's my own shop, and have a tidy round.'

She gave an exaggerated smile. There was a strong feeling of having to prove herself all of a sudden. The other workers really were a close-knit team, but until now she hadn't realised exactly how close.

'As long as you hold the fort — and selling as if it's your own sounds a good plan. If I leave now, we'll be back for locking up — we wouldn't expect you to do that yet.' Jeanie glanced at her watch. 'He'll be glad to get back, I think — it wasn't exactly the happy family party he'd been expecting.' She ran her fingers through her short, spiky hair. 'He'll never be able to leave his past behind, that's for sure. Not until he decides to speak his mind for once in his life — and I wouldn't want to be there if he does. Thanks for the coffee, by the way.'

Denise watched as Jeanie wriggled into her leather jacket and zipped it up. Then in one move, she gathered a diary and pen off the counter, popped them into the oversized bag and slung it onto her right arm, making for the door — but not before turning to flash Denise a look, one which reminded her of a cat, first in the queue for the cream.

Glad to be left alone, and thrilled to find herself in charge of the shop, Denise watched Jeanie wiggle down the street in her three-inch stiletto boots. She was protecting Craig from something or someone, that was obvious, and no doubt she wanted him for herself, otherwise why would she warn her off? . . . but what was it about his past?

* * *

The ringing phone distracted Denise from watching Jeanie's departure.

'Sadie, what's the matter? I haven't been here an hour yet.' Hoping nothing was wrong at home, Denise glanced at the clock.

'Forgot my sandwiches? I don't remember making any, and guess what? I'm running the shop today. Yes, just me, all on my own.' She couldn't help the smile that broke out across her face. 'And I met Jeanie. Yes.' Not wanting to voice her opinions out loud over the telephone, Denise heard that Sadie had to come into town anyway, so she'd pop in with some snacks later.

'That's brill, thanks. See you later.' She put the phone down and drew in a deep breath, looking round her little empire for the day.

Thinking of how efficient Maud

always was, Denise went to the cupboard under the stairs and selected two new rose and jasmine plug-ins. The floral aromas gave a welcome freshness to the shop, and she knew it made a difference in whether people lingered or not. She popped one in to the socket by the front door, and another towards the back wall.

Next, she took a duster and wiped off the fine film of dust she could see had settled on the centre display stands. Looking up the street as she flicked the duster across the window display, she saw the 766 pull into the bus station.

Only a handful of passengers got off, but there might be a prospective customer or two among them. Probably not the young lad with the rucksack, though and definitely not the elderly man, who waited while his dog cocked its leg against the nearby rubbish bin.

Determined to have the best day of the week so far, she opened the shop door and stepped out to admire the window display for a few moments, checking to see if there were any improvements she could make. Happy with what she saw, she made her way back into the shop.

She pegged the door open. It looked like being a fine day, and an open door was one less obstacle for approaching customers to think about as they walked through. Linda had explained that to her in the early days, and Denise had seen the difference an open door and a smiling face made to the mood of shoppers. She wondered for a moment how anyone ever came in when Jeanie was there. Then she remembered that Jeanie was more out and about than in the shop.

'Thank goodness,' Denise whispered.

Keeping busy was another tip from Linda. The thought of the bubbly little woman with the blonde, neatly styled hair made her smile. Such a bundle of fun — and Maud as well, though she was more refined, or tried to be, with her powder and perfume. It was never long before a joke and a smile came from her lips. They'd gone out of their way to make her feel really welcome.

You can't win them all over, she told herself.

She made slight adjustments to the straw hat on the mannequin in the window, put the swimwear in order of size, and placed the large bright-coloured sunglasses near bags of the same colour. The elderly man with the black Labrador, the one she'd seen stepping off the bus earlier, popped his head round the door.

'Can't come in, love, I've got Albert here.' He indicated to his dog, who Denise watched carefully, hoping her didn't repeat what she'd seen him do earlier. 'Only I want something special, and seeing as that's the name of the shop, thought I'd give you a try. It's Elsie's seventieth next weekend. She's always going on about some pasher . . . pashters, oh, what the heck was it?'

'Was it a pashmina?' Denise reached for the new arrivals of cotton scarves. 'These have just come in — and what a lovely present idea.'

Rather than risk him entering the shop and bringing Albert with him, she took three different patterned pashminas to the doorway.

'We've got checks, or black and white, or does your wife prefer more colour?' She splayed them out for him to look at.

'Elsie's not my wife, she lives next door. We're friends, and I wanted to treat her to a little something. She's good to me, bringing cakes and whatnot. Just thought it would be chance to say a little thank you. I know ladies like flowers, but she often has flowers. No, I wanted to splash out and treat her. Would the checked one be suitable for a seventy-year-old lady, do you think?'

'I'm sure she'd love it, and it's modern and light — feel it.'

He was reaching for his wallet before she'd finished talking. Looking slightly embarrassed, he handed Albert's lead to Denise.

'Hang on to that for a sec then, can you, love.'

Not wanting to interrupt the sale, Denise stepped outside and took Albert's lead, making sure to keep the other scarves well away from where the Labrador was beginning to sniff the air through the door of the shop. He turned away in disgust at the floral scents, and then spotted another dog across the street which he found to be far more interesting.

'Yes, she'll love that, when we go on our walks and weekend pub lunches. I'll take the checked one, thanks, love. Come here, Albert, sit down while I sort this out.'

Glad to hand the lead back to the owner, Denise took the note he handed her from his wallet.

As she nipped round the counter and wrapped the scarf carefully in tissue before popping it into one of the Something Special paper bags, she reminded herself never to make snap judgments on people and she'd made a sale, so it wasn't going to be a disaster of a day.

She handed the bag to the man, smiling.

'Thank you, sir — and make sure you pop back and let me know what Elsie thinks.'

'Oh, I will — she might come and show you what it looks like on. She's been in the shop a couple of times, maybe when you weren't here. That's if she likes it. Will she be able to change it if it's not right?'

'I should think so.' Denise crossed her fingers behind her back.

When he'd gone, she draped a couple of scarves in the window. If an elderly man who she'd written off as a definite no had bought one, then maybe someone else might, too.

The morning flew by, and when Sadie turned up with a pack of ham and mustard sandwiches, Denise realised how hungry she was.

'I'll make us a drink, if you keep watch for me — thanks.'

Glad of a break, if only for ten minutes, Denise told Sadie how she'd sold another three scarves that morning, from one man and a dog starting the day off.

'I'm not surprised — they're lovely.'

Sadie was finishing her coffee when Maud arrived.

'Oh, Sadie — didn't know you were here. I had a call from Jeanie. I've scrambled over to give Denise a break. It's awful if you're on your own and you need to have a few minutes. I won't stop though — only came to check she was going on alright and didn't want to phone, in case she had a shop full.'

Maud's familiar voice was slightly weaker than usual, Denise noticed.

'I thought you had a tummy bug? I'm alright; you should have stayed in bed.'

Glad to see her, but not wanting to get too close, Denise told Maud that Jeanie had put her in charge and it was turning out to be a good day.

'That reminds me, I've just heard that my niece is getting married in

August. Fancy having a go at making me a jade green . . . ' Maud put her scented tissue down on the counter and made a wide gesture with her hands against her already bouffant hair do. 'Would be good practice for you, and I might get something I really want rather than what's available, which is zilch.'

'Of course, I'd love to — but you get yourself back to bed. We'll discuss it when you're feeling better. Jeanie had to go and fetch Craig, apparently.'

Denise waited for Maud's response.

'Uh.' Her colleague raised her eyes to the ceiling. 'I don't know why he gets involved. His mother must have the worry of the world on her shoulders, poor duck.'

Shaking her head, Maud didn't say any more, and by then more people were browsing the racks of clothing.

It was Sadie who intervened, being the nosey and well-meaning landlady that she was.

'You'd never get through life looking

like that and not run into some raucous doings or another, would you?'

'It's not as if he invites it, though! And she needs to let him go, only that won't happen, according to what his mother tells me anyway.'

'His mother needs to let him go?' Sadie was speaking to Maud as if Denise weren't there, and by now a customer was calling for her attention.

She managed to hear Maud say, 'Not his mother, his long-time love,' before she walked to the other end of the shop. If she'd stayed near, she'd have heard Maud finish the sentence.

'In her mind, anyway. She needs to be told fair and square he's broken it off — only she won't take no for an answer, and he's far too soft and doesn't want to hurt her.'

Pushing away all thoughts of Craig and his long-time love, and Jeanie lining herself up to be the next one by the way she was acting this morning, Denise threw her efforts into helping a generously proportioned lady find a larger size than the one she was convincing herself she'd need.

'Pity it hadn't got a tangerine coloured hat to match — and there's no hope of finding one anywhere, I've already looked.' She walked to the counter, having tried on the size eighteen skirt suit, and being happy with the fact that it fitted with room for movement. Denise had taken a while to convince her on that detail, but in the end she'd decided she was right.

'Look no further.' Maud was still there, and Sadie as well. 'Denise is a milliner.' She winked behind the lady's back. 'She's almost finished the college course now, haven't you?'

From the way Maud worded it, she made it sound as if the millinery was the college course and she'd spoken up for her with such confidence that Denise didn't want to contradict.

'Had you a style in mind?' Denise couldn't believe her own ears. It might be one thing, making a hat for her friend, or one for Sadie and Joe for in the garden — now here she was taking orders as if she had her own hat business!

As she reached for the pen and notepad, it occurred to her that the way things were turning out with Craig and his string of love affairs, starting up in business herself to get away from him might not be such a bad idea.

7

'I've had twenty-five hits today so far, and it's only the first blog post.' Beulah swung round on her chair. 'If this is day one, imagine what it'll be like when I get really good.'

'That's fab — what did you blog about?'

'What I think will be in fashion for the season mostly, for the magazine I was telling you about, remember?'

'Of course I remember, silly. I do listen when you tell me things.' Denise pulled a face at her best friend.

'You're a bit quiet. Anything wrong? How's the dream job going?'

Not wanting to burden her friend, Denise shook her head. 'Everything's fine, thanks.'

Beulah's mother entered with pizza on a large tray with side bowls of chips and salad, a welcome distraction.

Denise had a feeling Beulah would try and wheedle every last bit of information out of her before the evening was out.

'I loved that hat you made for our Beulah. And if you don't mind me being cheeky . . . ' Mrs Struthers gave a sidelong look towards Denise before she continued, 'Tell me to stop if I am.'

'You liked the hat. How's that being cheeky?' Denise smiled and knew Mrs Struthers wasn't saying it to be polite. Known for her straight talking, she obviously meant it.

'I really would like one the same, but a bit different — and can you make it in a foxglove colour?'

'Anything's possible; they're my own designs, my own business.' Denise laughed out loud at her confidence. 'Is there an occasion you were thinking of? What about the outfit, and when would you want it?'

'Well, that's the thing.' She sat on the armchair between the two girls, absent-mindedly picking up a slice of pizza and nibbling the corner. 'I have the hat in mind, same as our Beulah's, only purple, and a bit wider brim, then I'll find an outfit to go with the hat.'

'Mum, that's a bit cart before horse, isn't it?' Beulah frowned, and Denise wondered whether Mrs Struthers was acting on a whim.

'Not really. The hat maketh the woman, haven't you heard that saying? We've got a thirtieth anniversary, so I'm going with a purple theme.'

Denise chuckled.

'I've heard *Manners maketh the man*. Something we did in English, wasn't it?' She looked towards Beulah who was engrossed in a magazine. 'Not sure about the hat one.'

'Then you'll need to get used to it, Denise. You can have it as your slogan, when you're known all around town and everyone wants you to make them a special hat. I'm opting for purple.'

Mrs Struthers rubbed her hands together and reached for a couple of chips. 'Mm, get on and eat this food, the pair of you, before I beat you to it. Don't forget, foxglove — the pinky-purple ones I mean, not the white ones. You know that lovely colour that's almost dusky.'

Denise grabbed a pen.

'I know, like the ones in the hedgerows round by Watery Lane.' She scribbled a note. 'Give me a week or so to look for the fabric. When is it for, did you say?'

'I didn't — not sure exactly, but it's later in the year. Any time you're ready though, I'll buy it.'

Helping herself to the food, after her mother had left the room, Beulah said, 'Hey, I've had this great idea. What if I put the hats on my blog? If we like them, then other people will as well. Would you mind if I did that?'

Denise frowned. 'Are you serious?'

'Never more so — they're good and you like making them, don't you?'

Denise let out a long sigh. She was feeling a bit mixed up. Maybe that was why she'd come over to her friend's house. If anyone knew her well, apart from Sadie — and she couldn't say too much to her landlady as she didn't want to burden her with things — it was her oldest friend, Beulah.

'Sometimes I think it would be lovely just to design hats and not have to go out and work for someone else.'

There, she'd said it — now for the twenty questions.

'I knew it. You've had a face like a wet weekend in Bognor all night. Come on, out with it.' Beulah pulled her chair closer and peered into Denise's face. 'They're not working you too hard, are they? It's usually right up your street to get your sleeves rolled up and get stuck in. Or is it something else?'

There was no getting away from the intensity of Beulah's bluey-grey eyes, especially when Denise hadn't been able to brush off her melancholy mood.

'I love the work, and the shop. The team are alright as well — close, you know? They treat me nicely, it's not that at all.'

'The boss is a bully . . . that it?'

'Nothing is *it*. Only me, feeling a bit sorry for myself, that's all.'

'It's not like you.' Beulah got up and enveloped her in a bear hug. 'Come on. Maybe it's time you found yourself a boyfriend?'

'Now you're starting to sound like Sadie! Honestly, I'm fine and certainly don't want a boyfriend. Remember the last disaster? I'm happy for you and Tony, and I do believe true love might find me one day, but now isn't the time. I'm going to be a hatter.'

'That's the spirit and you can talk to me anytime if anything is really wrong, you know that, don't you?'

'Of course I do. Thanks.' Denise, released from her friend's embrace, felt better, even though she couldn't put into words that she was feeling jealous. She didn't want Craig Spencer in her life as anything other than he already was — yet she couldn't help feeling envious of the spiky-haired Jeanie who was well and truly part of his world.

'I picked up a couple of hat orders from the shop today, and counting your mum's that's three.' Her mind raced ahead, making plans for the latest orders.

'Well, you could have told me when you got here. I think this is the start of something good.'

Knowing she had a friend to talk things over with made Denise feel much better.

* * *

Denise preferred wearing her hand-made skirts and knitted tops to some of the high street clothes that were on offer. Her dress sense was more boho and shabby chic than anything hanging on the rails. However she had her eye on a blouse she'd buy from the pastel range in the shop, when her savings could stretch to it.

Seeing customers enter the shop, looking for that certain something, not even sure what, then helping them choose an outfit and watch the transformation in their personality almost, always made her feel happy. Knowing she'd made a difference to that one person, and that the customer had left with a smile, made her realise how much she enjoyed working with the public. It gave her confidence in her own judgment and lately people were even waiting until she was there, to ask for her help.

The next time Denise saw Craig Spencer was on a Wednesday evening. She was in the shop on her own, working late. She'd come in at five o'clock to take over from Linda, who had left in a hurry. She wanted to cook Ronnie's favourite meal. He was due home following a week-long stay on the latest Tarmac job.

Linda had told Denise before she left how she'd placed an order for extra swimwear from a new supplier, and Craig was busy upstairs, going over the paperwork. He'd asked not to be disturbed, and that suited Denise fine.

When she heard his nimble footsteps coming down the stairs, she busied herself with draping light jumpers across a handbag display at the side of the shop. If he didn't want disturbing, she didn't have to look up.

'Hello, stranger, haven't seen you for a while. Everything OK?'

Denise turned to look at him.

Well, you have to admire the cheek of the man. It was perfectly OK for me to be spoken to like last week's chip paper by your girlfriend — one that you didn't think to mention when you were smouldering all of your gorgeousness in my direction.

'Really good, thanks, Mr Spencer,' she replied a little too chirpily. 'How was your weekend with the family?'

Arghh! She hadn't intended to say that. It kind of popped out and now she stood feeling a complete twit while fiddling with jumpers over handbags when they looked fine as they were.

'Oh, that.' He looked as if a thundercloud had burst over his head and left him soaked through. 'Let's say I'd be lying if I told you it went well.' For a moment his eyes flashed darker than ever. He ran his hand across the back of his neck and looked from left to right as if trying to rid himself of the memory.

'Tell you what.' He glanced at his watch. 'Why not put the closed sign up? There won't be many more shoppers around now, I don't think, anyway. Come upstairs — there's something I need to talk you about.'

Without hesitation, Denise turned the sign and bolted the shop door. Heart banging in her chest, she wondered whether she'd said too much. It was meant to be an innocent, polite question. He wasn't to know that she'd found out all was not well in Lincoln-shire.

When she got to the top of the stairs, she waited a few moments, then knocked on his door.

'I didn't mean for you to stand there. Come on in, Denise.'

From his tone of voice, she felt a stab of worry that her trial period hadn't been the success she'd thought. Was this the end of her time in his shop?

'We never did find time for a proper chat, after I came back from Paris.'

That was the last thing she'd expected.

'Well, you did tell us you enjoyed it.' She was being vague, but what was there to say? She was the part-time member of his team, the Saturday girl . . . who wasn't kept informed of much at all, from what she'd been finding out lately.

'Come and look at these.' He indicated a chair to the left hand side of him. 'Sit here.'

He flicked open a webpage and began to scroll down. 'Look at these. Thought you might be interested — I've been hearing how you've picked up a couple of orders.'

She stared blankly at him.

'The hat-making, Maud was saying.'

Craig's eyes were focused on the screen.

Denise recalled a day not so long ago when she had sat in this same room, heart beating just as erratically, only then not knowing a thing about the man sitting so close to her. Now she knew he was a heart-breaker. Trembling, she looked to where he was pointing.

'These are going to be big news. Hooded-type head gear, then there's the witchy-type cones.'

He really was serious. She was supposed to thank him and be grateful, was she?

'They look similar to the garden hats I've done for my landlady and a gardener friend . . .'

Yet however hard she tried, she couldn't get overly interested in the macabre images.

'Ha, you've already done these. That shows what flair you have, then.' He leaned back on his chair and studied her. 'I'm giving you an insight into what might be big later on in the year, and into next season.'

She'd heard enough.

'I'm not a copycat. It is thoughtful of you to show me these, but any designs I produce will be all my own. Not that I'd imagine seeing a witch's hat anywhere except at a Hallowe'en party! That's what I meant when I spoke about those paperclip dresses. They're equally hideous and unwearable, in my view.'

Denise glared at him and defied him to reply.

His face reddened and he sighed.

'I thought you'd be interested.'

He looked deflated, and she immediately felt sorry. What was wrong with her? His jean-clad legs were inches away from her. The rain pattering on the window matched her heartbeat and she began to feel much too hot.

'It's good of you to think that.' Denise cleared her throat and longed for a long cool drink.

'So, I thought you'd like to see the

hats, and you thought it was good of me to think that. Only you didn't.'

His sarcastic tone wasn't lost on Denise. She felt colour rising up her neck.

'There's another thing I wanted to ask you about — and this is more of a social event combined with work. I've got tickets to a fashion show. It's in London, at the Savoy. They do one every other year. I'd like you to come with me for this one.'

He rocked back on his chair and searched her face.

Taking a swallow and hoping he didn't hear the gulp, Denise wanted to scream, *Yes!! Yes. Of course I'll go.*

'Erm, can I have a think about that? Wouldn't Jeanie be the one to go with you?' Remembering the way she'd been warned off, the last thing she wanted was to be involved in a lover's tiff. 'She's your main, sort of, worker isn't she?'

Now her hands were trembling visibly and all she wanted was to get out of the room as soon as she could.

'She'll be there, of course. Maud isn't up to the travelling and Linda wouldn't leave Ronnie. I thought it might interest you, though, that's all. It's no big deal.'

So Jeanie would be there. And he'd given her a chance to go and see a real live fashion show in the Savoy Hotel, London.

'In that case, I'd love to go. Not sure how I'll get there, though. Train, maybe.'

She got up to leave, then swung round when he replied.

'I'll have the Jag back by then, so I'll pick you up.' Fishing in his desk he pulled out a couple of tickets. 'Here, keep these safe — and watch that landlady of yours doesn't snaffle one.'

Denise gave him an apologetic smile as she took the tickets from his hand. Knowing he was out of bounds made it more bearable to be in the presence of her boss and a visit to the Savoy would be something new. She couldn't wait to tell Beulah.

'What happened to the Jag?'

She really must stop blurting out these awkward questions, though.

'Someone decided to write their name across the side of it. Nothing that's not fixable. See you tomorrow.' He tilted his head to one side, and those blue eyes crinkled at the corner as he gave her a smile in return.

'Night, Craig.'

She ran down the stairs, her heart pounding and pressing the tickets close to her heart.

8

'I was thinking, if we get the old shed cleared out, you can have it as your workshop. Half the things in there are never used anyway. It's the greenhouse I'm more interested in these days.'

Sadie peered out of the kitchen window as she spoke. 'And don't worry, I'm not pushing you into doing more work. Just take your time. It'll be chance to organise all the stuff in one place, rather than having it dotted around the house — so you'll be doing me a favour.'

Buttering her second piece of toast, Denise looked towards her landlady in surprise.

'You'd let me do that? Sadie, that's something that's been worrying me lately. I've even been thinking of maybe having to look at storage units, like empty garages, places like that for me to rent. I'm so grateful.' Denise jumped up and gave her landlady a hug. 'This means I can buy more materials, and keep all the ribbons and feathers on display . . . if you're really sure?'

When Sadie nodded, Denise beamed.

'You have the answer to everything. It's not like I'm busy enough just yet to justify anything like what I had in mind.'

'Well, I can see you've had a lot going on in your head.' Sadie cleared her throat and gave Denise a knowing look. 'Only when I heard you've got more orders coming in, if you're going to do them properly — which you will, of course — then you'll need to spread out. It's not ideal with all the glue and bits and bobs hanging around in the house — and that way you'll have more privacy as well. I'll make a start on it today.'

'I'll find some boxes. If we do it at the weekend, we can do it together. Where will you put the things that will need to be kept, though? What about the lawn mower?'

Denise frowned, wondering if Sadie had really thought through what she was offering.

Sadie tapped the side of her nose.

'Ah, I've been chatting to Celia and Joe. He's offered to cut our grass at the same time he does his mum's, so we've no need to keep that old thing any more. He told me it's in return for the meals we pop round, so how could I argue with that?

'They said if I didn't agree, then they didn't want my cooking any more.' Sadie clutched her neck and made a shock-horror face. 'Heaven forbid, she loves a bit of shepherd's pie and told me my liver and onion is second to none. So, the lawn mower can go outside by the gate for the scrap pick-up van.'

'You're sure? Didn't Joe want it?' Denise felt responsible for all this upheaval.

'I've had it since Lord knows when, so no. He's got that petrol one, top of the range, so I doubt that ancient thing would be any use to him. Now stop worrying, and next time you're in the supermarket, have a look for any loose boxes if you want to do something useful.'

Laughing at the return of Sadie's normal bossy tone, Denise made them both another cup of tea. She waited until they were sipping the drink before broaching the subject.

'I've been invited to London. The Savoy Hotel — they're holding a fashion show.' She held her breath and waited for the questions to come winging her way.

Sadie, unusually quiet, sat looking at her.

'What? You're looking at me in a funny way.' Now Denise felt a chuckle building up and couldn't stop the laughter that was bubbling up in her throat.

'You're talking, so I'm listening.' Sadie smiled back, and they sat opposite each other, sharing a comical moment. 'Who would it be that's invited you then, love?' The tilt of Sadie's head and the look in her eye said she knew perfectly well.

Trying to sound casual, but failing miserably, Denise said, 'That would be Craig, my boss at work. He thinks it might be interesting for me. Only a works do — nothing special really.' She sucked her mouth in at the sides to prevent another smile breaking out. From the look on Sadie's face, she was presuming too much.

'You'll stop over, will you — or travel back the same day?' Her face was taking on a rather concerned look. 'Bet it'll go on into the night. These things usually do.'

'I didn't think to ask. The tickets are here — look.' Denise reached into her bag and pulled out the two large embossed cards, then passed them to Sadie. 'Jeanie's going as well; she's making her own way there, though. I presume she's got her own ticket. He gave me these to keep safe. What do you think, Sadie? Have you ever been?'

Sadie scanned the wording, and handed the precious tickets back across the table.

'I went for afternoon tea there once, when my Donald was alive. He took me as a treat when I turned sixty. It was so romantic. The pianist played in the background and we had a selection of sandwiches. He thought they were samples.' Sadie chuckled and then sighed.

Denise smiled wryly. 'I haven't been, of course. Those afternoon teas you speak of, they're more expensive than the cost of a night in a hotel anywhere else. Should I go? What would you do?'

Denise put her hands together with her thumbs close to her mouth, deep in thought.

Her phone beeped. After inspecting the screen, she announced, 'It's Craig. He's saying to pack an overnight bag as he's heard it's going on later than he thought.'

Sadie studied her lodger before she spoke.

'I've always felt like you're my family, you know, love. That's why I might sound bossy sometimes. It's only because I care. We were never blessed with children, Donald and me, as you know, and now it's as if I've been given a chance.' Sadie's eyes filled with tears.

Denise reached out and covered the old lady's hand with her own.

Clearing her throat, Sadie sniffed. 'Anyway, it's lovely to see you doing so well with your crafts. I'm proud of you and your mum and dad would . . . '

At the mention of her good friends, Sadie's eyes welled up again. 'Just be careful, that's all I can say.' Now her eyes were steady and she looked more solemn. 'Have fun, by all means, but don't hold on to any dreams that may come to nothing. From what Maud's been telling me . . . ' Sadie looked away.

'You haven't been gossiping about me?'

Denise knew that Maud had a hotline to Craig's mother, and Sadie wasn't on the back row when it came to hearing what went on around and about.

'All I'm saying is, please be careful. There's no room for broken hearts round here, and I definitely haven't got any Superglue that can fit those back together.'

'So you'd go, then?' Denise wondered if Sadie had even remembered her earlier question.

Sadie's twinkling eyes gave her the answer she wanted.

'Of course, you must go, but . . . ' Her gnarled arthritic finger pointed gently at Denise. 'Don't say I didn't warn you. Those good looks and charming manner come at a cost.' With a nod, Sadie got up and walked away. 'I'll be weeding in the garden if you want me.'

* * *

148

It was approaching midday. Craig had said to be ready by half past. Delving into the back of her wardrobe, Denise placed several items of clothing on the bed. What did one wear to a fashion show? Not only a fashion show, but one with work colleagues who knew lots more about up-to-date clothes than she did.

She wasn't aiming to look good for Craig — it was more that Jeanie would be there, and she'd be dressed to kill — in black, more than likely. Probably she'd look a million dollars. Denise sat wondering why she'd said yes.

For goodness sake, you'll look like the country cousin, there as court jester to keep everyone entertained, by making them laugh.

No good asking Sadie for advice, she'd made it clear she wasn't mad on the idea of her going. Beulah would think it was a hoot and loan her some way-out dress to wear if she'd told her, but she hadn't. She'd tell her about it afterwards, of course and they'd

149

probably laugh — it wasn't as if she'd lied, only omitted to mention it.

Now, keep calm, and breathe . . .

Denise closed her eyes and imagined herself, serene and happy, sitting next to Craig at the fashion show in the Savoy.

Right, that's it. The red dress, with the full skirt and belt pulled in at the middle. She reached up to the best end of her wardrobe, and found her old prom dress. It still looked good, and whenever she wore it she felt a bit special. That would be perfect. She was undecided whether to add her polka-dot scarf; that decision would need a bit of help from Sadie's critical eye.

'What do you think?' First she put the scarf on, tied loosely at the side. 'With,' then she whipped it off, 'or without?'

'Definitely with — looks lovely. Come here.' Sadie took Denise into her arms. 'You look fabulous. You need to get a move on and grab your strappy sandals, there's a man arriving outside.'

Whirling round to peep out of the front window, Denise watched as a navy blue E-Type Jaguar swung round and drew to a halt. Turning to Sadie, she gasped.

'I need to go and grab my overnight bag. Will you keep him talking? I won't be a second.'

She hurtled up the stairs, checked her hair then drew a slick of lipstick across her already glowing lips and batted her eyes to check her make-up.

'You'll do.' She gave herself a wink and an air kiss before making her way demurely downstairs.

Craig was handing Sadie a bunch of flowers. Mixed carnations, and not the kind you'd pick up in a garage or supermarket. A real bouquet of blooms, sprays and mixed colours. Gypsophila was mingled in there as well.

As Denise lightly kissed Sadie on the cheek, she remembered her words about charming and good-looking. Those gorgeous flowers covered the first part, and when she turned and looked into the eyes of her boss, her heart flipped. What price would she pay for spending an evening in the company of such a handsome man? Treading carefully in her high heeled sandals, the answer to that was one she was about to find out.

He opened the passenger door and adjusted a cushion on the seat. 'Watch when you get in, it takes some getting used to how low the seat goes.' His smile sent her heart beating faster yet again, and Denise wondered if she'd survive the weekend without suffering a heart attack.

As they sped smoothly down the motorway at what felt like a hundred miles an hour, Craig said, 'You look really lovely.'

His smile was friendly, not at all conceited. He'd made it clear that this was a business weekend, and yet Denise wondered why she was the one having a lift in the E-Type and not Jeanie.

Wondering what to talk about, she

remembered how much he worshipped his car.

'Did you get the damage fixed alright?' Immediately she'd said it she knew it sounded pathetic. Of course he must have got it fixed or he wouldn't be using it.

'Eventually, yes, thanks.'

'Vandals don't realise the trouble it brings, when they do something so stupid, do they?' She looked out of the window, watching the fields whizz past, and wondering how long it would be before they began to see signs of the suburbs.

'It wasn't vandals, just someone with a personal problem.' His grip on the steering wheel sent his knuckles white, Denise noticed, and his lips were pursed. She thought she heard his breathing quicken and could feel the anger he held towards whoever was responsible.

'Well, that's worse. Someone jealous, because you've got the car they want, you mean?'

He wouldn't thank her for delving. Turning to look at him, she decided to listen and stop talking.

'Something like that, yes.'

All angst left his face as he turned and met her eyes. Her insides turned to mush and she couldn't help wishing things were different.

Why hadn't she met him in some other circumstances? At a bar or in a club maybe, on a bus, or even in the park. Anywhere but at a stupid job interview. Would she have felt the same attraction? Surely he felt it, too?

He was like a giant magnet, pulling her close. She wanted to tell him to stop the car, jump across the gear stick and cover him in kisses.

Instead she nodded towards the sky and said, 'Looks like lovely weather . . .'

* * *

Craig pulled up outside a majestic hotel. Immediately a doorman

154

appeared and leaned down to his open window.

'Park the car, sir?'

'Thank you. We can manage the luggage.'

He handed his keys to the uniformed man, and leaning over into the back of the car, pulled Denise's holdall and his own sports bag swiftly out of the car. The man in top hat and tails strode round to Denise's side of the car. She nodded her thanks when he offered his hand to help her out of the low seat, unused to so much attention, but glad of the heave up.

Craig took her arm and led her through the grand entrance.

'It'll be nice to freshen up before afternoon tea. Hope you're hungry — they do a lovely spread.'

Remembering Sadie saying how her husband had thought the sandwiches were samples, Denise smiled to herself.

'Mm, I'm looking forward to it.'

She craned her neck to look round the foyer and take in the decor. Maud and Linda, Sadie and Beulah would be asking her what it was like later on and she wasn't great at keeping details in her mind unless it was to do with styles or fabric.

Then she looked at the back of Craig as he checked in. Firm shoulders, those black curls that would look far better if her fingers were entwined through them, sturdy legs — but not chunky — medium height, well-shaped derriere. She didn't have any problem keeping every minute detail about him in her mind . . . but only for herself. She wouldn't be sharing those details.

Her room was opposite Craig's — the most enormous room she'd ever stayed in. A television screen almost filled one wall. She had her own bathroom with complimentary robe, slippers, chocolates and mini bottle of champagne. Fresh flowers filled a vase, and the entire place smelled like lemons and limes.

Denise perched on the comfortable double bed feeling quite overwhelmed.

Whenever would she have even dreamed of staying somewhere like this? She was a working girl from a working class family. What a treat. She hugged herself and threw her body backwards to sink into the luxurious haze of what life might be like if she were married to someone like Craig.

* * *

'The others will be arriving later. I wanted to have some time to get over the journey. What do you fancy?' Craig's beautiful eyes met Denise's, and she had to bite her lip to stop herself from answering, 'You.'

'Salmon and horseradish? Or there's cucumber and cream cheese,' Craig went on, offering the platter of finger sandwiches to Denise. She decided on a couple of each. The flavours were exquisite and she wished she was bold enough to whip out a serviette and take some home for Sadie — but they wouldn't keep. She made a mental note to recreate them for her when she got back.

'It's so relaxing,' she remarked as she nibbled the delicate sandwiches, the like of which she'd never had before. 'I love the sound of piano music. It reminds me of when Mum played.'

The tea had a distinctive taste all of its own, and the scones and fresh cream tasted of heaven.

She sneaked a peek at Craig, who'd leaned his head back on the green velvet settee. He looked quite content, his eyes closed. All the anger from earlier was gone now, and when he opened his eyes and looked at her, he shook his head as if waking from a deep sleep.

'Sorry, almost nodded off there for a minute. It is nice, yes, very soothing.' He nodded towards where the pianist was playing. 'Are you looking forward to tonight?'

Denise felt her cheeks redden slightly as she wondered if he meant the actual night, or . . .

'The fashion show! — yes, so much. Where do they have it?' She felt immature and countrified at that moment, like a fish out of water.

'Mm . . . you've got the tickets, it should say on those.' Craig looked suddenly as lost as she felt. 'I'm not sure — there's a champagne reception, and then it's into the ballroom, I think. It's a charity do, but it's a good chance to meet up with the designers and mix a bit.'

He looked at Denise with an odd expression, as if he were quite happy sitting with her alone.

'Well there you are, you monkeys — trying to avoid us. Over here!' Jeanie appeared in front of them, gesturing to a group of people who were standing a little way off looking around. As Denise had surmised, she wore her trademark black pencil skirt and bomber jacket. Her immaculate hair and make-up gave her an almost alien look. For Denise, the perfect afternoon had turned to the beginnings of a nightmare.

'Shove up, you.' She hitched herself in beside Craig and planted a ruby kiss on his cheek, leaving a perfect pout on his face. 'Meet Denny and Minnie from In Scene magazine. I've been telling them about you. They'd like an interview later, and plenty of pic- cies . . . ' She took a chunk of Craig's cheek and pouted in front of him once more. 'And, you'll never guess. Back there, one of the models has asked who I'm with, and do I want to step in and have a go later. Imagine.' She swung round to make big eyes at Denise.

'It's all for charity, so why not?'

Craig looked irritated, Denise thought. Why did he let her get away with such behaviour? Treating him as if he were her puppy, or lapdog more like, the way she was mauling him at every opportunity.

When he jumped up, stretched his arms above his head and looked directly at her, Denise could have kissed him.

'Let's get some rest before the show starts. If you want to be fresh for later, then an hour relaxing will really help. These shows can go on for consierably longer than they plan to.'

Denise didn't dare look at Jeanie, though she wanted to stick her tongue out tauntingly. She couldn't believe it herself when she faked a yawn.

'Oh, good idea — see you later, everyone.'

Still she couldn't look Jeanie in the eye, but felt her disdain pierce her in the back as she followed Craig from the room.

When they reached the landing and Denise went to open her door, Craig took hold of her arm.

'Don't mind Jeanie — she's play-acting most of the time. She's like a sister.'

'A very close one! Here, she left a lipstick mark on your cheek.'

Denise reached up and wiped the red smudge where Jeanie had planted her mouth. Touching him made her heart accelerate all over again. They were so close, and all alone.

Craig reached out and tucked a lock of golden hair behind Denise's ear, then traced his index finger along her cheek.

'You look stunning today. Has anybody ever told you how special you are?'

She gulped and hoped he hadn't noticed.

'No, except family . . . is that what you meant?'

As she looked into the eyes that had captivated her from the start, she felt drawn to his lips. He looked with longing at her mouth and she couldn't believe it was happening . . .

They kissed for what seemed like forever, his arms circling her, holding her closer than any man had ever done. So close that she could feel his heart beating almost as hard as hers was.

Just when Denise was wondering whether he would end up in her room, that voice echoed up the landing.

'Craig, which room are you in?'

'Bloody Jeanie.' Gruffly he cleared his throat. 'See you in an hour.'

Denise escaped to her room and as she closed the door, she saw Craig nip into the room opposite. She could hardly breathe. Stuff Jeanie and her over-protectiveness. She'd just had a delicious, full-on kiss with Craig!

She slung her bag on to a chair, ran towards the bed and threw herself into its mound of soft covers. She gazed up at the ceiling with a great big smile across her lips. The taste of him was too nice to ever wash away.

Why did they have to bother with the fashion show when all she wanted to do was . . . ?

Oh, Sadie, what have I done?

9

The show was over. Denise stood, tingling with anticipation, for a good few minutes before she realised Craig wasn't coming back to her anytime soon. Feeling suddenly dejected, she unlocked her room, stumbled inside and, collapsing onto the sumptuous bed, closed her eyes.

The evening had passed in a whirl of colour, swishing fabric, clicking heels, frantic sketches, champagne bubbles and applause. Denise had taken in little of the show, conscious only of Craig sitting beside her and the heat of his body when his arm brushed against hers. Jeanie, caught up with her new friends and the thrill of being invited to model, left them largely in peace, though she had paused during her turn on the catwalk to shoot Craig a long, triumphant glance.

Much later, after they had made their way upstairs, once again Craig had drawn her into his arms and kissed her deeply and lingeringly in the hallway, their passions rising — until suddenly with no explanation, he had broken away from her and dived into his room.

It was over an hour later when she lifted her head, looked at the clock, then realised she hadn't undressed. She had been half-expecting him to surprise her — sneak in and tell her he couldn't get through then night without her.

Where was he? Not much hope of that happening now. Denise looked at herself in the mirror. Her mascara was smudged from wiping away tears, and her lips were a peachy red, not from lipstick but from the touch of his lips . . . Craig's soft, gentle lips, kissing her passionately, hungrily, as if she were the only girl that ever lived.

Then he had walked off.

He'd had quite a bit to drink — that's why he'd given her such a passionate kiss, she reasoned bitterly. Then when he'd woken up alone, he must have been annoyed with himself for not having swept her into his arms, taken her to his room and made her the happiest girl at the party.

Frowning at her reflection, she put her fists either side of her face, leaning her elbows on the dresser. *What did I do wrong? I thought he fancied me. What would be so wrong with an adult couple starting a relationship if they were attracted to each other?*

Frustratedly she pulled the red dress off and stood under the shower, washing all traces of Craig Spencer away.

She felt emptiness wash over her along with the delicately scented complimentary shower gel. Surely he wasn't waiting for her to go and surprise him? No, that would never happen. She may be a modern woman, but she'd been brought up to believe that if the man was interested enough, he'd make the first move.

Yet he had done — twice — and then . . . nothing.

What was it he'd said? 'I don't want to hurt you'? *He must think I'm a porcelain doll. He could at least have given me a chance to show him that I am capable of loving a man. It would be too easy to love him. I think I already do.*

Damn Craig Spencer and his high and mighty morals. She thumped the pillows and then picked up the remote control. There were plenty of channels showing late-night films, and she was in no mood for sleep. Several times she debated crossing the landing and showing him she was a modern woman, who knew what she wanted and didn't stop until she got it. She would sneak into his bed to surprise him . . .

Only pride stopped her. If he could walk away just when he'd made her heart race, and her body want him completely, then he could stay away from her for the rest of the weekend.

She peered into the fridge where a

selection of drinks awaited. Vodka seemed like a better option than going across the landing to jump on Craig. He could carry on with his life and she'd get on with hers, and forget about any more secret kisses on hotel landings!

She poured herself a drink, then added tonic and a chunk of fresh lime.

Denise was on her third glass of vodka and tonic with ice and lime when she settled back on piles of plush pillows to watch *Maid In Manhattan*. The film reminded her of what absolute idiots some men could be. She was asleep before it ended.

★　★　★

Next morning, a knock followed by a gentle rattling sound woke her. Denise shot up from her sanctuary of pillows, on her guard. No more kissing allowed! If all he wanted was a quick snog whenever he got the chance, then he'd need to learn she had more self-esteem than that — even though she would enjoy some fun. Her head had been stuffed with too many dreams of how life might be with Craig to take notice of Sadie's warning.

The breakfast trolley being shuttled into her room by the smiling young waiter was huge. She felt like a princess as he positioned it as near to the bed as possible, then lifted lids to reveal fruit, croissants and bacon and eggs. Pots of both tea and coffee were on the bottom of the trolley, along with sugar, milk and cutlery. The smart young man asked if she required anything else.

Denise shook her head and said, 'Thank you.'

He disappeared as discreetly as he'd come — like her very own Jeeves. She could easily get used to this kind of life and if it weren't for Craig she'd never have been here.

Mm, Craig. She really ought to thank him. Then she pulled a face as she recalled the rejection, after such passion, on the landing.

She swung herself out of bed, donned a robe and pulled up her chair to tuck into the wonderful breakfast laid out for her. As she placed the serviette on her lap, she couldn't recall ordering breakfast — nor even having a conversation about it. How strange. Perhaps Craig had seen to that as well?

The food was delicious, and the dull headache that had been lingering, she guessed, from mixing champagne and vodka when she didn't normally drink much at all, had completely disappeared.

Pushing the trolley to one side, she reached for a sheet of notepaper from the desk in front of her. The swirling letterhead looked impressive. Her own name was on the top — Denise smiled at such an extravagance, and knew she had to take that home in her bag. It wouldn't be of any use to anyone else, anyway!

She fumbled at the bottom of her

holdall until she found her pen. Making herself comfortable at the dressing table, she wrote:

Dear Craig, thank you very much for a lovely weekend. It was kind of you to give me a chance to attend a fashion show in such a beautiful venue. I hadn't been to the Savoy before. It's given me some ideas for when I make more hats and also it's a weekend I'll always remember.

Denise

Definitely no kisses; what would be the point? She wasn't going to lead him on, the way he'd been doing with her all weekend. She folded that page neatly, then reached for a second sheet.

So that's how you planned it, Craig Spencer? Kiss and run, then tell Jeanie how poor little Denise had been really grateful for the taste of your lips and the feel of your body pressing close to hers? That's your idea of fun, is it? If that's how you treat all the Saturday girls who come to work for you, then it's no wonder you find it hard to get the staff . . . and this is my letter of resignation. I no longer want to be on your team.

She screwed that piece of Savoy-headed note paper, with her name printed on the top, into a ball and stuffed it in her bag. He'd never see that one, of course — but it did make her feel better for having written it, even if she didn't intend to give up her job. Not yet. The first sheet was placed in an envelope with his name written on the front.

She showered again, to make the most of such luxurious surroundings as she probably wouldn't ever be here again. She dressed in faded jeans, a white cashmere jumper — her birthday present last year from Sadie — and flat denim pumps.

Taking a lingering look around her room, she stepped out onto the landing where she saw Jeanie and Craig chatting a little further along.

He looked up when Denise approached.

'Hi. We're just saying, Covent Garden

market is open. You'll love it — full of arts and crafts on Sundays. Did you have a comfortable night?'

Craig was bright and cheery considering he'd spent the night on his own. Or judging from the same smug smile on Jeanie's face, maybe he hadn't been alone after all. They were welcome to each other — in fact, they suited one another.

Denise held her head high and fixed a smile on her face. If they could act calm and collected, so could she.

'Fine thanks, breakfast was excellent. Did you have the trolley and room service?'

Determined not to show how disappointed she was at him leading her on, then dropping her like a hot potato, Denise pushed any thoughts of him being near her from her mind and considered the merits of Covent Garden.

'Yes, that sounds interesting — I might find something to take back as a souvenir for Sadie.'

Again she forced a smile as they made their way downstairs, and didn't feel guilty about all the toiletries in her bag. Everyone took those for keepsakes, didn't they?

'That's what I said to Craig; we'll need to take a present for Maud and Linda, or we'll never hear the last of it.' Jeanie interrupted the conversation and linked arms, fixing herself in between Craig and Denise.

Why did she keep saying 'we' all the time, referring to herself and Craig as a couple? She'd denied it and he'd tried to convince Denise they were only friends from a long time ago — but she wondered whether he was only kidding himself.

If he was that much of a wimp, then he wasn't really man enough for her anyway. She took a deep breath as they stepped out of the hotel and into the sunshine, feeling quite relieved that she no longer had to wish or worry about whether she and Craig would ever get together.

The market in Covent Garden was already bustling. Japanese tourists were busy taking photographs of a clown in striped trousers balancing on a unicycle. He looked at least ten feet tall. How had he got up there? Other visitors took group selfies, making sure the juggler was in the background of the shot.

Denise didn't want photographs to remind her of the weekend. She watched a mime artist who wore a bowler hat. His painted face and antics of trying to escape from a room with no door made her smile.

The craft stalls were bursting with hand-made scented candles and silk cushions. Plenty of traders were selling home-made fudge and chocolates. Denise was captivated by a display of fairy necklaces. Each featured a semi-precious gemstone, in the fairy's hands, corresponding to signs of the zodiac. She thought they'd make ideal gifts for Sadie and Beulah.

Her best friend would be so envious

when she found out about the trip and the fashion show. There was no way Denise would be able to tell her about Craig and his attempts to lead her on, though. She chose the amethyst fairy for Sadie, and the turquoise would be ideal for Beulah's December birthday.

Denise paid for her purchases, and had pushed them into her bag when a crumpled ball of paper fell on the ground. Only half turning to see what had fallen, Denise was horrified when Jeanie picked it up.

'You dropped this.' She rolled it round in her palm for a second before handing it back. 'Looks like rubbish, but you never know.'

'Yeah, only rubbish.' Denise laughed, relieved that Jeanie hadn't unravelled it and read out her letter of angry resignation directed towards Craig. He was behind her now and saw her looking at him.

'Did you get one for yourself? Those necklaces are really sweet. What's your birth sign?'

Suddenly reluctant to say when her birthday was, Denise was nonetheless aware that she had to travel home with Craig, and it would be a long journey back to Warwickshire if they weren't on friendly terms.

'I'm a Virgo.'

The guffaw from Jeanie couldn't be missed.

'You would be.' Then she must have had a change of heart. 'Sorry, couldn't resist . . . don't mind me.' She tottered along in front of them, her heels clacking on the cobbles.

Craig shot his eyes skyward.

'Can I treat you to your own souvenir? I heard you mention your landlady and friend. Please let me.' Gently he took her arm and turned back to the stall, where the silver-winged fairies, each with ruffled skirts and a gemstone in their palms, tilted forward as if to beckon all who passed by.

'I'll take one for the lady, please.' Craig pointed to the cascade of silver-plated fairies.

The middle-aged lady with blonde plaited, matted hair, wearing a rainbow-coloured, hand-knitted cardigan, smiled from behind the counter.

'You're back. When's your birthday, love?'

'Middle of September,' Denise said, shyly.

'You want the carnelian, then.' The stall holder reached over and unlooped a silver fairy with a golden-brownish stone from the tree where they dangled, sparkling in the morning sun. 'Would the gentleman like to do the honours?'

Denise wanted to laugh. Gentleman and honour in the same sentence to describe the kiss-and-run man who was her boss? Now that was funny. Still, she lifted her hair from the back of her neck while Craig secured the chain.

'You never believe that old tosh?' Jeanie had doubled back and stood with folded arms, smirking at the beautiful pendant that hung on Denise's chest.

'Ay — excuse me, if you don't believe in fairies, then step away from the stall.'

The seller wafted her hand to shoo Jeanie away. 'You'll offend them, apart from attracting bad luck. That'll be a tenner — thanks.' She was back with Craig and smiling as he handed her a note. 'You'll have all good things happen from now on.' The woman in the cardigan threw a dazzling smile towards Denise and then gave her a wink. 'Your fairy will protect you, but you have to believe. Carnelian brings joy and happiness.'

Denise thanked Craig, glancing over to where he was scanning the stall. She imagined he might be thinking of getting some fairy magic into his own shop. Business was never far from his mind, she knew that now. Even so, she looked down and couldn't help feeling a surge of happiness at the sight of the delicate nymph who seemed to be smiling up at her.

The market was like an Aladdin's cave to Denise, and she ended up with a selection of lengths of ribbon and fancy feature buttons, ones she knew she'd never find locally.

'Have you ever been in the Hard Rock Café?' Craig was asking her as if she popped into London most weekends. Of course she hadn't.

'We'll go for a cheeseburger. It's where we usually end up, isn't it?' Jeanie gave Craig a nudge. 'Oh, don't worry, they serve it with plenty of carrot and celery sticks. I wouldn't eat anything that's not healthy.'

'No, I've never been there.' Denise had heard of it, and seen it on the television once or twice.

They'd all bought everything they wanted. Jeanie's main purchases were organic beauty creams, and Craig had several bags of home-made chocolates. Jeanie hailed a taxi, saying she wasn't prepared to walk so far in those heels.

Denise turned away, wondering how, if Jeanie was such an expert on London, she hadn't packed some flats. It seemed a shame to be grabbing a cab when it was such a lovely day for walking.

'I've ordered you some tea. I'll drop Jeanie at Charing Cross, and then I'll be back.' Craig looked as if had a lot on his mind.

Nodding, Denise settled down to relax in the conservatory part of the Savoy.

Jeanie gave her a wave, and dragged her suitcase on wheels towards the entrance.

'See you back in the sticks.' Then she was gone. She wanted to call at Milton Keynes to see a friend, she'd said over lunch.

Denise poured the special Savoy blend of tea into the bone china cup, enjoying the moment.

She wouldn't be likely to have many more luxurious trips like this.

★ ★ ★

There wasn't so much of an awkward silence on the way back, more stilted conversation. Neither of them mentioned their kisses and Denise accepted that this weekend had been a business trip with work colleagues; nothing more.

Glancing down at her necklace, she was just a little smug that Jeanie hadn't been bought one. Then again, she hadn't wanted one. Nothing much about her was feminine. Perhaps that was what Craig wanted in a woman.

Stealing a glance at her boss, Denise knew she'd made the right decision to say yes to the trip — even though it hadn't ended as she wanted.

Halfway home, Craig pulled into a service station, saying, 'I need a coffee, how about you?'

'Yes — thanks.'

He strode off and Denise thought that, other than the gifts and the haberdashery items, she hadn't spent any money at all.

Craig came back with doughnuts and coffee.

'Thought you might be hungry.' He

passed her a bag. 'May as well finish with more junk — it'll be back to the gym and healthy eating tomorrow.'

He gave her a crooked smile through a mouthful of doughnut.

Denise noticed him tapping his phone, texting; someone else was after his attention, as usual.

'For pity's sake . . . ' He ran his hand round the back of his neck, as she'd seen him do in the shop when he was stressed. He turned to Denise, finishing her drink and cakes.

'I'll drop you off at home, and then I need to shoot straight off, over to Lincolnshire. It's Mum. She needs me over there — never a dull moment.' He attempted a smile, but Denise could see his mouth was set in a thin line.

She wished she could help, get him to talk, tell him it would all be alright. The rest of the journey went by in silence. It was obviously a private matter. If he wouldn't talk, how could she help?

At the end of the road, Denise gathered her bags. In her haste they tipped over, sending her packages spilling into the footwell. Hastily shoving everything back in, she thanked Craig for a lovely weekend, and handed him the envelope with his name on the front.

He looked slightly bemused. 'What's that?'

'A little thank you. It's been a lovely weekend.'

He smiled. 'I thought for a minute you were handing in your resignation.' He laughed as she hauled herself out of the low seat, and then gave her a wink as she slammed the door.

Neither of them noticed the crumpled ball of Savoy notepaper that had rolled under the seat.

10

'You really shouldn't go spending your hard-earned money on me, you know.' Sadie shook her head and drew in a deep breath as she draped the necklace through her fingers and held it high to take a closer look. 'It's really pretty, love. Thank you, but I didn't expect anything.'

She bit on her lower lip and a slight frown appeared across her forehead.

'Why shouldn't I? You spend most of your time looking after me.' Denise reached out and touched Sadie's hand. 'I really don't know where I'd be without you. You're my rock, but you know that, don't you?'

The elderly lady's eyes misted over, and then she sniffed, clearing her throat before asking, 'So, tell me more about the weekend, and the Savoy. You had a good time?'

'I can honestly say, one of the best.' Denise ran her fingers through her thick golden hair. She described her room and the afternoon tea with the piano playing in the background, just as Sadie remembered from her visit, then showed her the sketches she'd made at the fashion show.

Denise glanced at the kitchen clock.

'Beulah said she'd be here around eleven, to hear all about it. She's got a turquoise one of these.' Denise looked down at her own pendant and lifted the carnelian fairy to show Sadie. 'Craig treated me to mine. He said he wanted me to have a little reminder of the weekend.'

'That's generous of him. No hanky-panky then?' Sadie lifted an eyebrow.

Denise closed her eyes as she spoke decisively.

'No, none whatsoever.' She stuck her tongue firmly in her cheek and turned away in case Sadie saw the tint of heat on her cheeks.

'He's a gentleman, then. I thought

that the minute I saw him, standing there on the doorstep, asking to speak to you. You really don't get many like that these days.' She wrapped her fairy pendant back up carefully, in the tissue paper.

'Aren't you going to wear it?' Denise asked.

'I'll save it for special occasions — like when I go on my coach trips, or out for a meal, things like that.'

'I'm going to wear mine all the time. They're supposed to protect you; that's what the lady said who was selling them.' Denise patted her fairy and knew she'd never take hers off. Not even when she had a bath or shower. Well — maybe for swimming, as it might come undone and sink to the bottom at the deep end.

A hearty knock heralded Beulah, who opened the door and stuck her head through.

'Hi there, it's me.' She wiped her feet on the mat, then shook off her grey velvet pixie boots before rushing to

Denise for a hug. When she'd let go, Beulah opened her eyes wide and looked towards Sadie.

'My *best friend* gets invited to the Savoy, to attend a fashion show, and *doesn't think* I'd be interested?' Beulah clicked her tongue and exaggeratedly swivelled round to stare at Denise, before bursting into laughter.

'How lucky you are, Denise. You get to swank around in one of the top London hotels, see a fashion show, and get to meet all the designers and models and . . . Really, I'm not jealous. Well.' She squinted one eye and put her finger and thumb together leaving a miniscule gap. 'Maybe only this much — and to make up for not telling me before, you can give me all the details now.'

'It came out of the blue.' Denise felt awful telling a little fib, but she hadn't wanted her friend to be texting and calling every minute, which she knew would have happened if she'd told Beulah beforehand. Secretly she'd imagined a romantic time — which served her right for keeping it to herself and having such grand ideas.

'I'm kidding — we're not joined at the hip. Mum's got you another hat order, by the way. She was talking to Doris over the fence, as they do.' Beulah had pulled up a chair and joined them at the table.

Sadie busied herself organising drinks and sandwiches, then turned when she heard the hat news.

'Ah, that reminds me . . . While you were away Celia told me she's got a few boxes for you, ready for when we have that clear-out in the shed we were talking about for your workshop.

'Oh good, they'll come in handy.'

Sadie nodded. 'Joe's cat Smokey is due to have kittens over the next couple of weeks. Vera's been saving boxes to keep blankets and toys and food in. They've got more than they need. Joe told her about you transforming the shed, for making hats, and how we'd need boxes.'

'That's a cute name, Smokey.' Beulah laughed.

'It's from before Joe gave up the cigarettes. Vera called him Smokey Joe,' Sadie explained. 'Then when he came home from the allotments, with the little grey stray cat following him, it got nicknamed Smokey as well.

'Vera didn't want to keep the cat at first, but according to Joe, she's grown fond of her now. They're preparing for the big event. Celia's thinking of taking a kitten, for company.' Sadie placed drinks and lemon curd sandwiches on the table. 'She said to tell you, 'Pop round when you're ready for the boxes.''

'Can I help?' Beulah's huge blue-grey eyes lit up and her mascara gave the impression she was wearing false lashes. 'If you tell me what you need to throw out, and what to put where, it'll get done in half the time. It's not as if I've got anything else on. You haven't told me about the weekend yet either, so we can work and chat at the same time.'

'Well, I didn't have lemon curd sandwiches when I was little, but these are yum.' Denise wiped the corner of her mouth. 'It was like stepping back to another time. That's the best way I can describe it.'

Denise leaned her elbows on the table, cupped her face with her palms, and gazed into the distance. For a few seconds, she was back at the Savoy, with a handsome man whose kingfisher blue eyes pulled her close whenever he spoke to her, and had given her an awful lot of attention during their stay. Her thoughts jolted back to the present when she realised her two favourite people were watching her intently.

'Was the fashion show good?' Beulah asked.

'Really good, and it's given me lots of ideas. It's all in the notebook. We could make a start on the clearing today, seeing as the hat orders are mounting up. Is that alright with you, Sadie?'

Her landlady nodded enthusiastically. 'It's brightened up from that cloudy start. I'll get my gardening shoes on — we'll all muck in.'

Sadie wasn't one for shirking — and Denise knew that she, too, wanted to hear more about the weekend in London.

They had a break at one o'clock for orange squash and a scotch egg each with salad and crisps. Denise told them about the entertainers in Covent Garden as they sat in a circle on the canvas chairs, and about the stallholder selling the gemstone fairies.

'Oh, your present! I almost forgot.' Denise ran into the house and returned with the neatly wrapped gift. 'It's your birthstone — turquoise.'

Later, Denise prised the lid off a tin of paint with a screwdriver she found on a shelf. 'Yuck, it's all lumpy. There are a few more tins as well.' She looked at Sadie.

'If one tin's like it, they're probably all the same. Pass me a black bag, Denise.'

Sadie, now in full flow, hurled all the

old half-tins of paint into bags that Beulah said she'd drop off at the recycling centre before closing time.

'Argh! I've just walked into a cobweb.' Denise tumbled from the shed, spluttering and pulling at her hair frantically. 'Have I got a spider on me?'

She danced round in a circle, tugging and shaking her head upside down.

'Come here and stay still. You're not in the Hard Rock Café now, you know.' Sadie pulled a long-legged arachnid from the back of her hair and released it into a bush. 'There, all gone.'

Beulah was doubled up laughing.

'Sorry. It could have been a money spider. He'll bring you luck.'

'More like a monkey spider from the size of it.' Now Sadie was laughing with them both. 'Only teasing, love, we're bound to come across a few critters. It's ages since the shed's been sorted out like this. Phew, anyone fancy a sit down?'

Beulah offered to make coffee while they took another rest. Sadie shouted in through the back door.

'You'll find a cake tin on top of the cupboard. Bring that out as well, if you don't mind.'

Beulah didn't, and soon they were enjoying home-made fruit cake with the drink.

Sometime later, the old mower was wheeled up the path and left by the front gate, ready for the scrap man to collect. Sadie said it always amazed her how no matter what time she put items out, he seemed to come round the corner almost immediately, as if he had some inner radar.

In one of the cardboard boxes collected from Celia next door, Beulah had placed ant powder, fly spray, Jeyes fluid and other chemicals. Sadie had made room for those in her utility room. She had a cupboard housing only dozens of used carrier bags, so they fitted in there nicely.

Gardening gloves, plant food, spray bottles and all her plant labels and seeds, Sadie put under the aluminium stand in her greenhouse, arranging them tidily in another of Celia's boxes.

The modest tool kit kept for emergencies would stay in the shed. Denise didn't want to force every last thing out of its usual place, and she'd need a tool shelf anyway.

'It's going to be smashing. I can just tell.' She smiled and gave her landlady a warm embrace. 'I'll work really hard — thank you, Sadie. You've gone out of your way to help me, with all this space.' Denise threw her arms out and twirled around the now empty shed.

'I think we've worked wonders.' Beulah stood back and admired the clear space. 'I'll come and give you a hand to clean it next week.' Glancing at her watch, she picked up two bin bags. 'If I go now, I'll catch the tip before it shuts.'

'Let me . . . ' Denise took another two and helped her friend fill the boot of her purple Ka.

When all of the bags were loaded up, Beulah turned to Denise. 'Look, why don't I stop off at the chippy and bring us something in for tea? Sadie's supplied snacks and drinks all afternoon.' Beulah nodded to where their hostess was brushing away remaining debris in the back yard. 'I'm starving, and it would finish the day off a treat. And you *still* have more to tell me about the weekend — I can tell.' With a cheeky grin, she jumped in her car, and beeped as she started the engine and pulled away.

Denise laughed, suddenly feeling quite hungry herself. Apart from that, she felt as if she was moving on to a new phase in her life.

She wandered down the garden. The shed needed a thorough clean before she could fill it with her materials and hatting equipment. She'd run up some curtains, and then it would be ready for her to move in. The future was looking brighter than it had done for some time.

She looked forward to starting up her new business, but for now she planned to carry on working in the shop, and build up her trade slowly.

When Beulah arrived back with fish and chips for three, they feasted and chatted until late.

★   ★   ★

The first thing Denise had bought for her new workshop was a strong padlock and key.

'I found this in The Toolshed in town.' She proudly fished into her bag and produced the chunky item.

'You're right to be on the safe side, it's going to be your livelihood of hats wrapped up in our little shed. I'm so proud of you. Any ideas for a business name?' Sadie studied her crossword as she spoke, then looked up.

'Well, I did like World of Hats, but that's a bit ambitious — and there's already a hat maker using that name.' Denise chewed on her thumb nail.

'Oh, I see.' Sadie took her glasses off and offered a suggestion. 'What about

Happy Hats?' Then she went blank. 'Oh, it's harder than you think to come up with something good and original, isn't it?'

'Then I'll go for the obvious.' Denise sat up straight. 'Mullsey Hats. As far as I know there aren't any other places called Mullsey in the country. And it's where the idea began — here in your kitchen.'

Sadie beamed. 'Yes! And from the workshop in the back garden to — ' she flung her arm wide — 'Greenland, Japan and the rest of the world.'

Denise was laughing at Sadie's optimism.

'I'll make a sign for over the door when it's been cleaned out.'

*　*　*

It was during a canal walk, two weeks later, when Denise stumbled across the rugged slice of bark by the edge of the tow path. Using Sadie's wood burner that was among the tools, she etched

Mullsey Hats into the wood with the hot iron. The result was slightly wobbly, and the sign hung a little crookedly, but it looked creative and unique all the same. The green and white checked curtains that hung from wire across the windows were made from remnants she'd found in Sadie's bit box. Denise tied them back using narrow yellow cord. The whole effect gave a sunny feel to her new workplace.

Before long she was up and running with the hat making. From the window of her workshop, Denise could see blue tits hanging upside down on fat balls, and sparrows feeding from the bird table. A robin sat on the back of the bench, trilling a merry tune, and keeping her company as she busied herself with the latest order.

Scents of Sadie's flower border drifted through the open door of the shed. Tubs of sweet peas in delicate colours and contrasting giant blue delphiniums swayed in the summer breeze. When she looked up the garden,

Denise could see her landlady, stooped over, busy weeding.

The electrical supply had taken a while to organise. Joe had a mate who'd recommended someone he knew who was properly qualified, from the building trade. He put in several sockets so that Denise could listen to her favourite radio station, as well as having the facilities for the steamer and her laptop.

It was a balmy summer evening when Beulah phoned.

'Don't tell me you're still hard at work?'

'I didn't start until late. How's things?'

'Really good, thanks. Ascot was fantastic. Shall we pop out for a drink? Then I can tell you all about it. Tony's working late tonight — only we haven't had a girly chat for a while. How about I pick you up and we go to Boadicea's wine bar, grab a bite to eat and relax for an hour or two?'

'That sounds like an offer too good to resist.'

Denise was smiling as she closed the shed door and secured her workplace. Life really was good these days . . . so why did it feel as if something were missing?

★ ★ ★

The wine bar was busy for a Thursday night, with a few couples chatting intimately in the alcoves and several jovial groups enjoying a joke from the sound of it. Denise bought the first drink, as her friend refused her offer of petrol money. They both chose black-currant and lemonade; the ice and slice of lemon gave added zing.

'How's your blog and website going?' Denise felt slightly guilty that their conversations had been all about her recently. She had almost forgotten that her friend was settling down with her new job as well.

'Mm, it's OK . . . Not taking off as well as I hoped it would.' Beulah studied the menu and took a sip of her drink. 'I fancy the triple loaded pizza.' She grinned, looking up at Denise. 'The diet will continue tomorrow.'

'Pizza's healthy, isn't it?' Denise kept a straight face. 'Think of the vegetables, and olives . . . and tomato is known for having zero calories, isn't it?' She nodded earnestly, then chuckled. 'I really feel like the home-made chicken pie.'

She pushed the menu aside, and went to order the food. Shuffling back into her seat near the wall, and making herself comfortable, Denise placed the small sachets of sauce and condiments in between them on the solid oak table.

'So what's the problem with your online work?'

She listened as her friend explained that she'd been busy writing articles and gathering information about fashions and latest trends, but not amassing as much income as she had first thought, even though she'd known all along it wouldn't be megabucks.

'I did enjoy it, but somehow the

interest has gone. Not from the blogging and website stuff — it's the fashion industry. It all seems a bit fickle and false to me.' Beulah's eyes had lost the sparkle they normally held. She pursed her lips and looked as if she'd made a secret confession. 'Now you hate me, because you're getting deeper into it and I'm not so sure.' She sighed. 'Sorry to be a wet blanket — this isn't why I suggested coming out.'

Denise could have kicked herself. She'd known Beulah for years, and she'd been too wrapped up in hats and other things to spot that her friend was feeling so despondent.

'I'm the opposite. Computers aren't my thing and I'm dreading having to build a website for Mullsey Hats.' She grabbed Beulah's hand. 'I know . . . You could do that side of things for me!'

She looked up as their food arrived but continued as they tucked into the meal, 'I won't be able to pay a fortune, but it would help me so much if you could set up the website and start me off with a blog.'

'You know how to do all that yourself — don't say it to be kind.' Beulah looked embarrassed.

'I can, but I'm rubbish and I need all my time to be creative. The shop job is taking up more time now, too. They get me to cover anyone who's off, and busy spells — which is good, but my time's better spent working with the hats.' Denise held out her hands. 'Well, at least if you get it set up for me, I'll give you a one-off payment. I need a techie person and you're one, so . . . '

'It would be more interesting . . . and I could take a lovely boho photo of you in the doorway of the workshop for your home page.' Beulah's melancholy moment had passed, and the twinkle had returned to her eye.

'That's an idea.' Denise was glad they'd come to an arrangement. 'Then if I need, say, a once-a-month communications person, I'll know where to come.' She smiled. 'So, come on, how was Ascot? Did the hat stay on, by the way? It was quite blustery from what I saw on television.'

When Beulah had finished telling her about the amount of compliments she'd had on the trilby, they both ordered chocolate fudge cake with ice-cream for dessert.

'When you think about the future, where would you like to be in five years from now?' Beulah savoured a melting chocolatey mouthful.

Denise had no hesitation.

'I'll have my own shop, of course. Mullsey Hats will be known all around the county, or country . . . no, around the world.' She sat up straight and thumped the table. 'I'll have a room where I'll run workshops as well. If Mullsey was once the town of hats, there's no reason why it can't be again.' Shocked at her own outburst, Denise gave a throaty laugh. 'Well — if I can't have faith in myself nobody else will.'

Beulah agreed. 'I think it's marvellous, and I'll do the techie stuff for nothing if it means you affording equipment, materials and things.'

Shaking her head, Denise reached for her bag.

'We're in this together. You've helped me a lot, from asking for that first hat to spreading the word. Now I've got a pile of orders. Without you and Sadie, I wouldn't be having a chance to build something from nothing.'

As they got up to leave Boadicea's, she patted her middle. 'Yep, the diet starts tomorrow.'

* * *

Saturday morning in the shop was no different from any other weekend, apart from being busier than normal. Busier for Denise, that is. Before eleven o'clock, she'd filled a page in her small notebook that she kept under the counter.

'It's really lovely to see how popular your hats are,' Maud said. 'It's like you're bringing the craft back. I hope you won't be leaving us.'

Denise felt a bit embarrassed, thinking back to her chat with Beulah in the wine bar. Not guilty enough, though, to stop her taking details and phone numbers from ladies wanting to order a hat for their special occasion.

Craig had come from upstairs, and was wearing a frown as he marched purposefully through the shop. He'd caught the tail end of Maud's question. Denise could have slunk under the counter.

'What was that? You're getting more orders, I've heard.' He was telling rather than asking, and he didn't look enthusiastic. He turned towards them. 'I wanted to talk to you about that if you've got a minute.' He retrieved his tuna pasta salad and a bottle of energy drink from the fridge in the kitchen, then marched back upstairs.

It was clear from Maud's face that she'd caught the urgency in his voice as well. She looked at Denise, who was standing wondering if this was the moment she would be leaving the shop.

'Good luck, love. I'm sure it's something and nothing.' She smiled encouragingly.

Denise took a deep breath and made her way upstairs, wishing she could stop her heart hammering like a tin drum in her chest.

He was in his chair, the other side of his desk, and Denise hesitated before sitting down opposite. He swung his opened laptop round to show her a series of hats being paraded down a catwalk.

'Now, I know I've shown you these before, but they're the latest designs from Stephanie Goshen, and they're selling faster than doughnuts off Brighton Pier.' He nodded to where the dome-like Gothic creations were replicated on each waif, looking quite ridiculous, she thought.

'You're doing this to make money, obviously?'

His face was almost unrecognisable from the relaxed, enthusiastic man she had spent time with in London. He'd changed from being a man who made her insides turn to melted chocolate into a hard-nosed business man.

Why was he taking so much interest in her enterprise idea? She needed to put him straight.

'I don't like those.' She shook her head. 'I'm making what people are asking me for. Real people who live in Mullsey; they're folks I know. They trust me, because I listen and create the best hat for that individual person.'

'I wasn't suggesting for you to be anything other than your creative self, Denise.' He smiled wearily. 'And I don't think you understand. I want to help.' He leaned back in his chair and it looked as if the energy had been sapped from his body.

'Look, I know there were parts of the London trip that may have been . . . ' He searched for the right words and gave up. 'Let's say, I'd definitely like you to attend the Paris fashion show, later on in the year. You really should go to as many as possible to see what's out there. I'm not trying to be rude, but you have to look further than Mullsey High Street and your own back yard. It's a small world now — the opportunities are out there.'

Did he know about her workshop? From the way he was talking about back yards and business opportunities, he probably did. No doubt Sadie had been talking to Maud, who might have mentioned it to his mother who happened to be one of her best friends.

No wonder he knew so much. Denise had to stop herself from smiling so she sucked her lips together and pulled them in.

'What's the future plan, regarding your hat business? I know you're getting more orders than you have time to make, according to what I've heard — especially with the extra hours you're putting in here, for me.'

His question threw her completely, and his penetrating gaze sent her into panic mode.

'I haven't made a set plan yet.' She

crossed her fingers under the table to compensate for the lie. 'You're right about having more orders than I can make, but working here helps with the money for buying materials, and the trip to London gave me some good ideas.'

Heat rose to her face and she wanted to escape. Dryness filled her mouth and she felt like a rabbit trapped in headlights.

'I . . . think Maud might need a hand, if you've finished showing me — ?' She pointed to the screen where faceless matchstick women, or girls, or things, pranced like zombies up a catwalk.

As she got up to go, his face looked quite crestfallen.

'The offer is still on, for a trip to Paris, in the autumn,' she heard him say as she turned.

She swung back round to look at him.

'I'll think about it, if that's alright. I'm not sure what I'll be doing yet.'

'It's a works trip, obviously.' Then he gave her a smile that made his eyes crinkle at the sides and she melted inside.

'Obviously.' She turned and left him to his dodgy hats before he had chance to catch her extra-wide smile.

★ ★ ★

It was half an hour before closing time. An attractive lady with long, blonde, wavy hair stood outside, absorbed in the window display.

'Wonder if she needs any help?'

Denise craned her head to see if the browser might be a potential customer.

Maud glanced up from her word-search puzzle, her little treat on a Saturday afternoon, and then disappeared into the kitchen.

The browsing lady suddenly marched into the shop, her iPhone in one hand, showing off long false nails and clutching a designer handbag. She walked around the shop looking up at the higher shelves and down towards the shoe rack, before running a finger along the handbag shelf.

Wandering from rack to rack, she slung clothes from one end of the rail to the other, and then spun round to face Denise.

'Is Craig in?'

'He is. Can I be of any help? I think he's busy.' She smiled, feeling an odd chill down her neck.

'I'm Cynthia Barton-Hays, and whatever he's doing, it's not as important as a visit from his fiancée. Tell him I'm here, will you?' She looked down at her phone, flicking the screen a few times, before glancing back up at Denise with a pout of her bright pink lipstick.

She did a marvellous impression of a model, swirling round with a swish of her hair and prancing to the other end of the shop to start rearranging the window display.

11

Knocking on Craig's office door, Denise opened it gently when she heard him say, 'Yes?'

'Your . . . erm . . . it's . . . ' the words were stuck in her throat. She swallowed hard, but it didn't help. 'It's your fiancée . . . she's downstairs.' She spat the news out, quickly closed the door then ran back down to the shop.

She couldn't bear to see his face light up at the news. How could he forget to mention being engaged? Perhaps he didn't think she'd find out.

Cynthia was quizzing Maud, obviously already fed up with messing the window display around.

'Margie, no . . . Maddie? I met you in Grantham, at Craig's mother's, didn't I? When his grandma died, that was it. You were at the funeral, helping

Barbara with the sandwiches. I remember now.'

'No, I'm Maud.' The older woman looked warily at Cynthia.

'Ha ha, whatever.' She wafted her hand as if to dismiss the conversation. 'I always say to Craig, his mother and her friends all look the same. Kind of . . . '

Footsteps could be heard on the stairs, and Craig entered the room, in time to catch Cynthia's rude remark. He finished the sentence for her.

'Glamorous is the word you're looking for.' He directed a wink at Maud, who smiled back at him. 'You'll be alright closing up for me?'

Seemingly Craig was telling rather than asking. Maud nodded.

'Craig, babe, I don't mind helping with the cashing up.' She fluttered her long, fake-looking lashes and made a point of positioning her long nails on the till in readiness, and then as he approached, she pounced.

'I wanted to surprise you. You're always too busy working, so I just hopped on the train.' She draped an arm round his neck. 'I've booked a table for two at the Malt Shovel, it's your favourite place for food, and I bet you haven't been eating properly. Well, I'm here now and if I'm going to be taking over the running of the shop for you, I need to get used to working the till.'

She studied the huge computerised machine as if it were some foreign object.

'There will be some changes that I need to discuss with you, by the way.' She gave Denise a sidelong glance as she spoke.

Her look sent Denise cold. Her face was frozen into a false smile which she suspected looked as hideous as she felt. Where had this awful creature come from? Lincolnshire, obviously; and from the sounds of it, planning to move to Mullsey when they married.

Craig's face had gone ghostly white. It must be a bit embarrassing for him, having his wife-to-be appear when he hadn't ever mentioned her once.

Affording Cynthia the merest glance, he said, 'Come on, leave my ladies to run the shop, they're more than capable.' Grabbing his car keys from the usual hook, he ushered her out of the back door without speaking another word.

Denise and Maud heard the engine start up and then a few minutes later, the cloud of blue disappeared up the High Street.

Maud spoke quietly for once.

'Now there's trouble if ever I saw it, cheeky madam. Barbara's been at her wits' end lately, poor soul.' Maud turned the sign to *Closed* and pulled down the blinds. 'You can help me cash up, love. We'll be quicker that way.'

'I didn't even know he was engaged.'

Denise didn't want to ask, but she had to know more about the woman with wavy blonde hair and curvy figure. She looked quite fake — not Craig's type at all. Then again, she hadn't known him that long. What *was* his type?

'Don't get involved, if you want my advice, love. Keep out of it, that's the best we can do. He treats us well, he's a good man, so let's leave them to it.'

Trying hard not to cry, Denise knew now there was no hope of getting together with Craig and only moments before, he'd invited her to the Paris fashion show. There was no hope of going now, and that was an awful shame. She'd decided as soon as she'd walked out of the room that she'd say, *Yes, I'd love to go — thank you for asking me.*

She'd really been looking forward to it, but more than that — the notion of spending a weekend away, in Paris, with her gorgeous employer, would have been a dream come true. Now she had been reminded that wonderful things like that happened only in fairy tales . . . not in real life, and certainly not in hers.

Joe had cut the grass and trimmed the hedges in Sadie's garden. She'd produced a huge jug of homemade lemonade, and Denise joined them both for a refreshing drink when they'd all finished their afternoon's work. Sadie had tidied the borders, busy weeding and hoeing; Denise had orders to complete, in the workshop, and Joe had been doing the heavier jobs. They'd been chatting and catching up on each other's news for over half an hour, when he glanced at his watch.

'Well, better make a move. Vera's finishing work a bit earlier today, so we're going for a bar snack.' He stood up to go. 'Tell you what. Why don't you both pop down? We're only going to the Owl and Compass. You could meet us in there.' He glanced up at the cloudless sky. 'It'll be a lovely evening in the beer garden. I can pick you up if you decide to come — text me, Sadie.'

Then he looked at Denise. 'Talking

about the hats, while I remember, our Vera's been going on about ordering herself one. You could tell her how you're getting on; have a bit of a chat. It'll save me trying to tell her what you've got, and I'm not sure she even knows what she wants.' He cast a warm smile in Denise's direction, gave a cheery wave with a grass-stained hand, and left, trundling his petrol mower along behind him.

After they'd both showered and changed, Denise and Sadie decided to walk to the pub. The Owl and Compass wasn't far, and they didn't want to put Joe out.

'It's a lovely evening, and there's nothing nicer when it's like this than being out with friends, is there?' Sadie said, raising her glass of shandy to her friends. They'd found Joe and Vera sitting at a table in the back garden. It overlooked rolling fields and row upon row of oaks and sycamore trees. The pub gardens were packed.

Denise ordered scampi, and Sadie

decided on the same. Joe and Vera had already put in their order for quiche with salad and skinny chips.

Vera wanted to know more about the hatting venture Denise was building up, and she invited her to call at the workshop.

'Ring first, to make sure I'm there,' she said. 'That way you can look at what I've done already, and then see if anything comes close to what you have in mind. If not, I'll make something to order for you, and I can measure you up.' She smiled.

'Now why didn't I think of that?' Vera chuckled. 'Mind you, I've been up to my ears in furry little friends recently. Did Joe tell you, Smokey had her kittens?' She looked at Sadie and Denise.

'I knew there was something important I should have said.' He shook his head. 'We were all so engrossed in talking about the garden, delphiniums, lupins and Denise in the workshop, it slipped my mind.' He gave a half laugh.

'Sorry . . . We've decided to keep a couple. She's named them Sooty and Sweep.' Joe sneaked a glance at his wife. 'Mum's going to have one, and that leaves one to find a home for.' He raised his bushy eyebrows and looked thoughtful. 'Don't suppose you'd fancy one, Sadie? To keep you company.'

'I've got Denise to keep me company. What are you saying? That I'm a lonely old lady? If I wanted a pet, I'd get a dog.' Sadie gave Joe a scolding look but from her smile it was plain to see she was joking with her old friend.

'How about you?' Joe said to Denise. 'Imagine how a little kitten would love to curl up under the workbench while you do the creating. You wouldn't even know she was there.'

She smiled and didn't say yes or no. It might be something she'd be interested in, but she'd talk to Sadie privately first. It wasn't her house to bring a pet into, but the thought of a fluffy little friend to make a fuss of did sound quite appealing.

When they left for home, after refusing a lift again from Joe, Sadie and Denise promised they'd join Vera and Joe more often at The Owl and Compass during the summer months.

'It's been lovely catching up. I'll give you a call when I'm a bit more organised with these kittens,' Vera said.

The following Thursday, Joe's van was parked outside his mother's. Sadie had been busy making her famous beef lasagne.

'He's been so good, and never asks for anything in return. I know they both enjoy a pasta meal.' She wiped her hands on her apron and nodded in satisfaction, then wrapped a clean tea towel round the tasty offering. 'You don't mind popping that round for me, do you, love?'

Denise found Celia and Joe in the front room. They were watching two of the cutest kittens she'd ever seen, gambolling around on the floor.

'Hello — Sadie's sent some lasagne

round for both of you. I've left it in the kitchen.'

'Oh, that's really kind of her. She does spoil us. Thanks, love.' Celia looked up and gestured for Dense to sit down. 'I'm having the boy one. Joe says they're less trouble than the females.'

Celia had a twinkle in her eye. She was dangling a ball of pale blue wool and watching the two little bundles of joy tumbling over each other.

'I've been trying to convince her that two kittens are better than one.' Joe grinned. We've already kept two, as I was telling you. Our Vera says that's more than enough, and Smokey is recovering nicely. She's a protective mother; would have kept them all if it had been her choice. She wasn't too happy to see these leaving, but I told her they weren't going far.' He had a smile on his face just like any proud father.

Denise couldn't help but smile at him.

'How sweet are they?' The smallest

one sprang up like a wind-up toy and bounded towards her. 'I've never seen kittens this colour. I must go and fetch Sadie — she'd love to see them.'

A few minutes later, Sadie gave a half knock and walked in. Celia's living room now resembled a small child's playroom.

'Oh, they look like a bundle of fun.'

'We're looking for a home for this one. She's the last one I was telling you about.' Joe bundled the one with white-tipped toes into Sadie's arms.

After fluffing its ears and saying, 'Oh I'd be frightened of treading on the little love,' she handed it to Denise.

Something about the way the kitten looked at her with big blue eyes melted her heart.

'Couldn't we have this one?' She looked expectantly to where Sadie was now pulling a cotton reel on a string along the floor for Celia's new pet.

'I'm happy with one of them.' Celia beamed. 'I've told Joe, two would be a bit much for me to manage.' She tickled her kitten, which was chewing the tassels on her slippers.

'Don't feel pressured.' Joe rubbed his hand across his brow and looked a bit embarrassed. 'I only brought these round for Mum to see.' He looked to where the brother and sister were chasing each other round the settee. 'I wouldn't have asked, only now you're here and what was that about your lasagne then, Sadie?'

Joe was powerless to resist when it came to Sadie's cooking. Vera was too busy to cook from scratch and he said he didn't mind, but he never refused Sadie's home-baked meals.

'Well, I don't mind if you want to take care of the kitten, as long as you know it's yours — and I don't have to clean out the litter tray.' Sadie winked at Celia as Denise scooped up the tiny creature and cuddled it to her chest.

'Of course, I'll look after her completely. She'll keep me company while I'm working in the shed. And,' she beamed at Celia, 'they'll be able to see each other, being neighbours.' She cuddled the kitten and placed her gently back on the carpet. 'Have you chosen a name for yours, Celia?'

'I think Charcoal, along the same lines as Smokey, his mum. And you? Bit soon, maybe, you've only just found out you're having one.'

Denise sneaked a glance at Joe.

'Well, I might have been thinking of getting one.' Denise fondled the kitten's ears as it jumped across her lap. 'She's going to be Cinders. When can we take her, Joe?'

'Now if you like, unless you need time to get a few things together. I can drop you off some food and a box. You'll need a couple of blankets, and cat bowls. You can always borrow some of ours until you get some. You know what Vera's like,' he smiled. Always gets four times the amount of stuff we ever need.' He lifted his eyes skyward. 'Love her to bits though, and she'll be chuffed as ninepence to know you've had the other one.' Joe beamed. 'You know how she tries to be firm, but she'll still be able to see them with Mum having Charcoal, and you with Cinders.'

'How much, Joe? I forgot to ask,' Denise said.

'Don't insult me — I'm only glad they're going to a good home. It was unexpected, to say the least. I thought I'd gained one tomcat. We're going to make sure it doesn't happen again, though. Smokey will be paying a visit to the vet.'

Whistling, he walked into the kitchen and began dividing the lasagne between two plates.

* * *

Denise was in love with her new baby. Even better, her brother was only next door and they were sure to be playmates.

'Cinders, the little last one of the group, who nobody wanted. You remind me of myself.'

She reached into the cardboard box,

lined with one of Sadie's crocheted woollen blankets, to give her some fuss. Cinders rubbed her head up against Denise's hand.

'You understand my feelings, don't you?'

Two blue, loving eyes fixed on Denise, almost hypnotising her.

'Little beauty, you're so precious, and I have a little secret. I think Sadie adores you as well. Do you know what she did yesterday?' The kitten tilted its head to one side. 'She came back from the supermarket with that premium cat food, even though you're too young to eat it.' The kitten purred with delight at all the attention. 'She'll spoil you more than I will, you'll see.'

The kitten gave a huge yawn, showing a tiny pink tongue, and then curled up in a ball. Denise opened a window to let fresh air into the workshop. The kitten was good company, and she didn't regret the decision to take her on one bit.

'Oh, look at this.' Sadie fluffed up the newspaper she'd picked up in town earlier. Cinders, curled up on her lap, only lifted her head when the paper accidentally knocked into her.

'Sorry, little poppet. The building that was once used as a hatting factory is being restored and made into flats.'

Denise came in and sat down next to her.

'Well, we'd heard about the developments, hadn't we, but listen to this . . .' She read aloud how there would be a few units that would be available to artists and craftspeople as shops. Mullsey Council were open to offers, and plans were being considered later in the year.

'Only whoever applies for a shop . . . da di da di da . . . ' she flitted past what she must have read as jargon, then said, 'It would have to fit in with the town and the history of the building.'

Gently Sadie placed Cinders onto the floor.

'Reasonable rents, for suitable applicants.' She sat back and took off her glasses.

'Are you thinking what I think you're thinking?' Denise looked at Sadie and chewed on her bottom lip. Her imagination was roaring into top gear. Already the shed was too small for the work she needed to do.

'Well, it seems like an ideal solution to your space problem,' Sadie replied. 'Don't think I haven't noticed how cramped you are in there, and you've got more work coming in every day. I know because it's lovely to have people calling at the house. Quite like old times at the factory.'

She handed the paper to Denise, who scanned the news item and then reached for a notebook and pen.

'I'm going to give them a ring.' After a moment's thought, she changed her mind. 'Better still, I'll pop into the council offices. There might be a few people making enquiries. If I have a chat face to face, then it might give me a better chance.'

Denise was determined. Her business was expanding and all along, she'd wanted to bring hatting back to the market town of Mullsey. Getting a shop of her own — and in the actual old hat factory! — would be a way of pushing herself forward. She felt slightly apprehensive, but excited. She would make enquiries first thing tomorrow.

12

Denise heard her name called after waiting fifteen minutes. She was in the old building that doubled up as a police station, council office, Job Centre and Citizen's Advice Bureau. She made her way to the vacant cubicle and sat down opposite the clerical assistant.

'How can I help you?'

'I'd like to put my name down for a shop in the old Hat Factory, please — when it's renovated, I mean. I saw the article in the paper saying they're going to be available, for local crafts-people.'

Denise sat up straight, holding her head high, showing off her jade-green creation that went so well with her honey-blonde hair. She spoke firmly and with confidence.

The clerical worker reached for a form. 'I just need to ask you a few questions before we can process your application.' She gave a stilted smile. 'What is it you intend on doing there?'

'I've started up a hat-making business. I'm working from a garden shed at the moment.' She took her hat off to show the woman. 'This is one of my designs — I brought it to show you.'

Unexpectedly, nerves began to kick in, with a slight trembling in her hands, and a feeling of tension building up deep inside. She really hoped her slight apprehension didn't show. It felt as if she were opening up her soul and putting her heart on the line waiting to be judged.

Denise cleared her throat. 'It's getting cramped in the workshop. I have so many orders coming in, I need more space for the hats. That's the gist of it.' She'd promised herself she wouldn't waffle.

Get right to the point and speak plain English. She sat back and watched the lady sitting opposite tick and write in boxes using the information she'd given. It had crossed her mind that with the interest Craig had shown in her hat making, he might have let her display them in his shop window. She could have let him have them at a discounted price. What an easy option that would have been. Free advertising, and ready customers already coming into his shop.

She didn't want to burden him with her new enterprise though, and he might think she was giving them to him. Or he may want to say no, and feel obligated. Either way it would complicate matters ... and his fiancée certainly wouldn't agree to anything like that. That's why she needed to be independent and find her own shop.

'We'll be able to let you know in a few weeks, and if your application is passed, then we'll show you round and sort out a date for handing over the keys.' She patted the forms and then glanced at her watch. 'Is there anything else?' Now her smile was more relaxed.

Denise took the printed page the

clerical assistant had provided. It indicated the amount of Council Tax and rent that would be due by direct debit each month, should she be successful, and all other details about the property. Her plan was to carry on working at Something Special and get the shop up and running on her days off.

'No, I think that's all — thank you.'

She so wished they could tell her yes, or no, right now, and not keep her in suspense. The next few weeks would feel like an absolute age.

Denise was bursting to tell someone. As she left the office, she rang her best friend.

'Are you free for coffee? I have some news.'

★ ★ ★

'That's so exciting . . . ' Beulah gasped and gripped Denise's arm. 'Imagine, you'll be able to do a proper window display and you could sell accessories as well like lace, ribbons, buttons, all that kind of thing. You could have it as a milliner's cum haberdashery shop. I bet Sadie's pleased, she'll have her shed back.' Beulah laughed.

'She's more than pleased; it was Sadie who noticed about the shop units in the paper. She's already told me I can still use the shed as a home base. Probably use that for any dyeing and planning when I'm not in the shop.' Denise bit her lower lip and smiled. 'Listen to me; I'm talking as if I've already got it. I've just got to wait a few weeks now.' She pulled a face and rested her chin on the back of her hands.

'What do your work colleagues think about the news?' Beulah asked.

Denise had just taken a mouthful of coffee. She coughed and pulled a tissue from her pocket.

'I haven't told them yet.' She looked up under her lashes, moved her eyes slowly sideways to the left then right, as if checking to see if anyone nearby had overheard, and then stifled a smile.

'Imagine if I get turned down? I'd look like a right muffin. They know I'm making lots of hats, though, so it wouldn't be a surprise. I'd rather wait until I know for sure, and then break it to them gently. When do the exam results come out?' Denise took a more ladylike sip of her coffee. 'It feels as if all we do is sit around and wait for things.'

'Not long now. I know what you mean. We're ladies in waiting. How do you think you've done?'

Denise shrugged. 'I don't know, and I'm not sure about ladies . . . ' Denise wiped coffee off her blouse, and reached over to point out that Beulah had dropped jam from her doughnut on her top.

'I'm not too sure either,' Beulah said. 'But as long as it's a pass, Mum and Dad will be happy.' Beulah covered her mouth with her hand. 'Sorry, didn't mean to sound flippant. It must be hard for you, and with all the excitement of the shop. They'd be really proud of you. I am.'

'Don't be sorry. I'm alright. Sadie is brilliant, and I've got you.' Denise smiled. 'Where would we be without our friends?' She gathered her things, and told Beulah she needed to call in at the supermarket for a few bits and pieces for tea. She'd promised Sadie she would cook tonight.

'I'm making salmon with lime, ginger and chilli marinade. Thought Sadie might like to try some Thai food.'

'Sounds yum — what time do you want me round?' Beulah joked.

'I hoped you'd say that, just in case she doesn't like it. She won't let on if you're there.' Denise grinned. 'Give it a couple of hours, and it'll be on the table.'

Denise stood up, brushing off Beulah's protests about not having been serious.

'Be there, or I'll know you're not really a friend at all — only an impostor who just wants to spread all my hot gossip to your mum and the horsey crowd at the stables where you go to play 'Hooray Henrietta' sometimes.' Beulah stuck out her tongue and Denise laughed as she turned to leave. 'See you later. I don't mind if you tell your mum. Just remind her to keep it to herself.'

The meal turned out to be tasty, if completely alien to Sadie's experience. Normally she would cook salmon with new potatoes, green beans and parsley sauce, as she pointed out.

Her verdict was, 'Yes, tangy, and exotic, but I wouldn't want it every week.'

Denise had smiled at Beulah, knowing that if her friend hadn't been there, Sadie may not have been so diplomatic.

★ ★ ★

'We'll have the new clothing range over near the window.'

Craig was making more of the decisions lately in the shop, and didn't mention Cynthia's visit. Every time Denise went in to work, she half expected her to be posing behind the counter, or teetering down the stairs in her heels, but she didn't appear . . . until the following Friday.

Jeanie was working late with Denise. Craig was upstairs. All was peaceful and calm, until the door banged open. If a world war had broken out, it couldn't have been worse than what came next.

'Craig! Are you up there? I've been cleaning your car out and you'd better explain this . . . '

Cynthia was holding up a scruffy-looking piece of paper, shaking visibly, her normally immaculate face looking like someone who'd spent too long in the sun.

Denise caught the word *Savoy* on the familiar paper and her heart sank.

Oh my goodness me, where can I hide — or should I run out now, before I get involved?

Too late, she already was in deep water.

'Jeanie, what's been going on around here? You're my friend! You should have told me and — ' She squinted, and then focused on Denise, like a lioness catching sight of a gazelle. 'You must be the author of this little sonnet.' Her eyes blazed, she began breathing deeply and advanced menacingly. Denise took a step back.

For the first time since she'd known her, Jeanie had a look of fear on her face.

She whispered, 'I did try to tell you. What's on that note?'

Denise's lips would not move. When Craig appeared, she didn't know whether to be glad or even more worried. At least he'd saved her from having her hair torn out, she guessed.

Her heart hammered as she watched.

The fiancée stood, pout exaggerated and hips akimbo, glaring at Craig as he scanned the rumpled page.

Denise felt as if she might be sick. She'd meant to burn the note on Sadie's fire, but after she returned from

London, she wasn't able to find it.

In his car . . . of all the places, and his fiancée finds it.

Well — she really needed to hear that she'd got the shop in the Hat Factory, from the look on everyone's faces right now.

Her plan was to grab her bag and run. Then Craig spoke.

'Jeanie, Denise, that's it for today, thanks. I'll see you both in the morning.'

'But I haven't finished!' Cynthia turned and pierced Denise with another ferocious glare. 'If she's trying to worm her way into your bed — '

'Goodnight, ladies, and see you both when you're next due in.'

They were out of the shop in minutes. Denise walked as fast as her feet would take her to the corner of the street. Jeanie was a few paces behind her.

'So what was on the note?'

Jeanie wasn't going to let it go, and Denise knew there was no point denying or hiding anything. If she was a friend of Cynthia, she'd soon find out.

Lifting her face skyward, Denise sighed.

'When we were at the Savoy — ' She felt so embarrassed she didn't want to go on.

'Yes. You and Craig went up to your rooms when you'd finished your afternoon tea — anything to do with that? Mrs Madam is riled — something's upset her and believe me, it doesn't take much. I tried to tell you.' Jeanie folded her arms and looked up and down the street, and waited.

'I'm stupid, that's what the note is about.' Denise couldn't lie, and didn't want to make Craig out to be a groper, because he wasn't. 'In my mind, I thought something might happen between us, and Craig would try something on — but he didn't.' She hoped that would satisfy her because if Craig destroyed the note, maybe she wouldn't hear about the kisses. That would be too embarrassing — and there was no point in repeating every last word she'd written.

'It wasn't meant to be read by anyone, it was only me having a private rant.'

Jeanie nodded. 'I can see there's some spark there, and that's why I tried to warn you.' She shook her head and closed her eyes. 'Why did you plant something like that in his car?'

Denise huffed. 'It must have dropped out of my bag. I wrote it in my childish temper, and that's all it was. Believe me, Jeanie. He didn't tell me he had a fiancée. I'm not a marriage wrecker.'

'I know.' Her prickly colleague smiled. 'And, hey, he said see us both later in the week, so let's try and forget about it, eh?'

Denise nodded and gave a tiny smile. That was alright for Jeanie to say. She wasn't the one having to face the boss with egg on her face.

Perhaps she'd ring in sick . . . but she couldn't avoid the situation that was out of her control now anyway. She'd face the music, either way — and wear flat shoes, just in case she needed to run.

* * *

Mullsey Library was a hive of activity with a poetry reading in one section, rhyme time in the children's corner, and a family tree research tutorial for those looking up their ancestors.

Denise wanted some quiet time, and soon realised she'd come to the wrong place when a crocodile snapped its teeth and the youngsters screamed. Guitar music accompanied the lilting poets; she sat and listened to that for a while, before browsing for an escapist read.

She found a chunky book by Maeve Binchy, one she hadn't read. It was through reading Sadie's books that she'd discovered the Irish writer with the ability to transport her to another world. That would keep her mind busy, and stop her wondering what had happened after she and Jeanie had left the shop.

A poster on the wall caught her eye.

Ghost Watch at the Old Hat Factory Moving closer, she read the small print. Before the renovations were completed, builders and local historians wanted to hold an all-night Ghost Watch, and anyone interested would be welcome.

As soon as she left the library, Denise texted Beulah, who was always up for some fun.

★   ★   ★

'Of course I'll come, but I don't think we'll see any ghosts.' Beulah was far too grounded to believe in anything other than the here and now.

'Yes, but imagine all the workers from years ago. Surely there might be something.' Ever the romantic, Denise wanted to believe. 'Sadie, you worked there, did anyone . . . you know?'

'What, drop down while they were on

the job, you mean? Of course not. It might have been hard work, but they didn't actually work us to death.' She chuckled and shook her head.

'Would you like to go, Sadie? You never know, there might be an appearance of someone you'd remember, who's passed over.'

'I'm knitting you a jumper for the autumn, and it won't knit itself. You go — and then you can tell me all about it when you come back.' Sadie patted her hair, looking pleased to have been asked. 'I know I'm a young sixty-seven, but spending the night in an old factory isn't my idea of fun.'

Denise chuckled. 'You'll come, then,' she said to Beulah. 'We'll take a flask and sandwiches.'

Beulah nodded. 'I wouldn't miss it for anything.'

★   ★   ★

It was a Tuesday when Denise was next at work. She was with Maud, and it wasn't long before the conversation came round to ghosts, and the night at the hat factory.

'You know I'd love to go back — even if only to have another look round. Is Sadie going?'

'No, I couldn't convince her, she doesn't want to.' A vision of blue flashed past the shop and they heard the engine of Craig's car purr around the corner to his usual spot behind the shop.

'Thing is, they've been renovating. You'd think the best time for a ghost hunt would have been before the builders had started work.'

Craig walked in on the ghostly conversation.

'Ghost hunt, did you say?' He had a twinkle in his eye. Denise thought he looked gorgeous. What a waste that he was engaged to Cranky-pants Cynthia.

'Yes, the old hat factory. Why don't you come, Craig? Imagine if some ghostly apparitions appear! You'll be like Scrooge in that film . . . 'I didn't do it, it wasn't me.'' Maud teased.

'Who else is going?' He was in the kitchen putting his lunch in the fridge and making coffee.

'My friend Beulah and I thought we'd go and, well, see what appears. There'll be some of the builders who've been doing the work. I think they've heard some odd bumps, and wanted to hold a ghost hunt before the work gets finished. They haven't fixed a date yet.' She shrugged and gave a sideways smile. 'Should be interesting, but I wouldn't have thought it was your thing.'

'It's not something you go around saying, is it? I believe in ghosts.' Craig looked at Denise's fairy necklace, glinting in the morning sunlight. 'My grandma's cottage, the one in Wales, was definitely haunted, but it wasn't anything to feel scared of. Just something we grew up with.' He smiled. 'I'd like to go — if only to be nosey and look round the old factory . . . feel the atmosphere.'

'That's what I said,' Maud agreed. 'Hey, maybe we'll end up on telly, like Derek Whatsit and Yvonne Doo-dah.'

The doorbell tinkled, a customer entered and began browsing. Craig went upstairs, saying, 'Make sure you let me know when it is.'

Maud went to ask if the customer wanted any help. Denise chewed on her bottom lip and fiddled with her carnelian talisman, wondering why Craig was suddenly coming to a ghost watch. What had he done with Cynthia Cranky-pants — or did he intend to bring her as well?

★   ★   ★

Denise waited and watched for the postman every day, eager for news of her shop application.

'He'll think you've got a thing for him, the way you rush out every morning,' Sadie laughed.

'As if I've got time to have a thing for anybody.' Denise flicked through her order book and crossed off another dozen hats that had been delivered the week before. 'It's that I'm getting more and more orders. It would be so much easier if I had more space. It feels like I'm intruding on your privacy with people calling at all hours. It must get on your pip a bit.' Denise looked at Sadie and sighed. 'It shouldn't be long, but I'm not sure what's going to happen if they say no.'

Sadie put her knitting to one side and leaned forward. 'There isn't any point in worrying about something if you don't even know yet. I meant to say this before. Don't you go worrying about paying rent here and on the shop, if you get it. You're bound to make a go of it; I can see how well you've done since moving everything over to the shed. You'll do even better when you get a little property. I'll back you all the way, and if you need help for say, six months or so, then put me down as what do they call it? Executor, guarantor, whatever it is, I'll be it.' She picked up her knitting and carried on with her purl row.

'You'd really do that for me?' Denise felt sorry for making such a fuss. 'There's no need. It's up to me to sort all that out. There's something else I meant to tell you.' Denise breathed out slowly, wondering how Sadie would take the news.

'There's a room — or two rooms — above the shop, so it could be turned into a flat if I need it to. Not that I want to move out, or anything.'

She glanced nervously at the woman who had been as good as a grandmother to her since losing her parents. The last thing she wanted was to hurt her feelings, but she wanted her to know.

'Well of course it has. I guessed as much.'

If Sadie was bothered, she didn't let it show.

★ ★ ★

'All ready for tonight?' Denise could hear the excitement in her friend's voice as she trilled down the phone during her lunch break at work. 'You'll never guess. Tony wants to come as well.'

'Tony wants to go to the ghost watch?' Denise looked at her co-workers and smiled. 'That's great. The more the merrier. Craig is coming as well.'

Maud whispered to Linda, 'Are you going?'

The bubbly blonde shook her head.

'No, me and Ronnie are having a quiet night in.' She giggled. 'I've bought some things from that new underwear range we've had in.'

'Blimey, and your mum as well? There won't be any room for the ghosts.' Denise laughed into her phone. 'Oh, alright, I'll tell her. Maud, Beulah says her mum will pick you up if you like. She and Tony will come and fetch me.'

The conversation covered what snacks

they'd be taking and whether to stick to non-alcoholic, or otherwise with the drinks.

'Yes, we need to be sober if we're hoping to pick something up.' Craig appeared, and gave her one of his charming smiles just at that moment. Denise felt her cheeks flush.

The day came to a close, and Denise waved goodbye to Maud who wanted to go straight home for a bath and get ready to face the spirit world in the building where she once earned her living. Linda, clutching the bag containing her new lacy underwear, shouted 'Ta-ra' as she ran out to Ronnie's waiting truck exactly on five o'clock.

Craig cashed up the till, while Denise cleared the counter and swept the kitchen floor, gathered bits in a dustpan and emptied it into the bin. She swilled the cups and placed them to drain.

'Looking forward to tonight?' he casually asked her, leaning on the kitchen doorway, looking tanned and more handsome than ever.

'Absolutely.' Denise beamed. 'Are you?'

'It's something I've never thought of doing, but yes, in a strange way, I am. And I was thinking . . . Has Maud got a lift? I meant to ask her before she left.' He tilted his head upward and tutted.

'My friend Beulah's taking me, with her boyfriend. Her mum is picking Maud up. It's all arranged. I'll see you there, then.' Denise reached for her handbag.

'If I picked you up, they could save on petrol and use the one car.' He leaned his head to one side and Denise felt that familiar somersault flip.

'Well,' she frowned and put a finger to her lips. 'Wouldn't your fiancée have something to say about that? I've already been glared and growled at, and about the note . . . '

He placed a finger on her lips.

'You don't have to explain anything, except maybe to your friend. I'll pick you up at seven.' He held the door open while she slipped her light jacket over her shoulders.

She knew she ought to demand an explanation, but everything about being with Craig felt right — as if they were two halves of a whole. She knew that was stupid. He was engaged to someone else . . . Or was he?

13

Denise didn't want to let Beulah down. She'd always been there for her, but she really wanted to accept the lift from Craig. When she heard the knock, and Sadie welcoming him in, with plenty of time to spare, she made the call.

'It came out of the blue, he offered me a lift at the last minute, and so I thought if you wanted to all go in the same car, there would be room for you to take your mum and Maud, without me.'

'Oh, that's nice, of course it's alright. We'll see you in a while. And don't forget, you promised to bring cheese and pickle. I've made fish finger and brown sauce sandwiches.'

Beulah didn't make a fuss. That was one of the things Denise loved about her. She never questioned anything and really was a true friend, but before she rang off, Beulah said, 'You can talk to me, you know, about him — if you need to.'

Feeling heat rush to her face, Denise was glad they were on the phone and not face to face.

'About . . . err, him?'

There was no fooling her friend. She would tell her sometime, but not just yet. There was nothing really to tell.

'Ha, listen to you. Look, I'll have to go, I'm still not ready and I need to wash my hair. See you down at the factory. Enjoy the ride.' Beulah's laugh was infectious.

'I'm just showing the young man your shed,' Sadie hollered up the stairs, and before Denise could reply, they'd disappeared from the hallway.

She looked through her bedroom window. A few minutes later, they came into view. Craig seemed to be listening intently, his head to one side, glancing at Sadie now and then. He was taking time to admire flowering shrubs and plants that Sadie was pointing out.

Oh my word, she's telling him the name of every flower in the border from the looks of things. Denise had a mini-cringe and hoped Sadie wasn't saying anything too personal. Her landlady did have a habit of saying whatever popped into her head.

Next they made their way across the lawn and down the gravel pathway, and stopped outside her shed. Sadie fiddled with the keys and then pulled open the door. They disappeared, and Denise realised she ought to be getting ready, not ogling the rear view of her boss.

It might have been better if she personally had shown him round her workshop, but she knew Sadie couldn't help herself — and she was a good help when it came to dealing with people who turned up unexpectedly to talk about, or order, hats.

Pulling on her faded jeans, Denise leaned back on the bed to zip them up. All the homely cooking was starting to show on her waistline — the diet would start on Monday. She selected a summer vest, and a cream, fluffy angora jumper with cowl neck completed her outfit. She slipped her feet into her tatty trainers. There might be rubble around, or loose floorboards. No point getting too dressed up. She noticed Craig wore his ripped jeans as well, with a rather scruffy-looking jumper.

She pulled a brush through her wavy hair and tried to smooth it down, without luck. After applying minimal make-up, she glanced out of the window for the second time. They were making their way back up to the house.

Taking a deep breath, she hurried downstairs.

'That's a fantastic set-up you have.' Craig looked her up and down. 'Your workshop is amazing. I hope you didn't mind, we took some pictures.' He blushed slightly and Denise thought he looked really cute. Like a little boy caught with his hand in the biscuit tin.

'No harm in that, is there?' Denise laughed.

'I told him it's alright, lovey, he said

he can print them out for you and . . . '

'Yes, it's all digital these days, Sadie.'

'In my day, you'd have to take a film in to the chemist and then go back two weeks later. Oh, my word, how things have changed.' Sadie appeared to drift off on a wistful moment, and then jolted herself back to the present.

'Listen, love.' She swung round to face Craig. 'He's made a suggestion, haven't you?'

Craig was smiling, and had that familiar twinkle in his eye as he looked at her rather intently.

'You could have a corner of the shop for displaying them, if you liked.'

Now Denise's heart began to beat faster and she hoped — no, prayed — that Sadie hadn't told him about her application at the council office. She tried to act cool, but her hands were sweating and she wanted to get out of the cottage as soon as she could. For one thing, she had to ask him about Cynthia . . . but not in front of Sadie.

'That's a good idea,' she squeaked,

then cleared her throat.

'No obligations. Have a display and then you'll get more orders. They really are special. You must be proud.' He was looking in Sadie's direction.

'She's worked hard. I couldn't be more proud if she were my own granddaughter.' Sadie folded her arms across her chest and looked taller than her five feet, two inches. 'She'll go far, trust me on that.'

The look she gave Denise told her that she hadn't let on about the shop in the factory.

'Perhaps I could bring one of each colour, in different designs. If you're sure it's alright?' Denise could hardly look at him, and hoped he wasn't just trying to be kind. 'We should make our way now, I think. I've made sandwiches.'

'There are two flasks . . . one tea and the other coffee. You'll be there most of the night I expect. Oh, aye, spending the night together and not even married.' Sadie chuckled. Denise grabbed the bag of refreshments and kissed her lightly on the cheek and escaped from the cottage. As they disappeared down the garden path, Sadie shouted, 'Don't worry about Cinders. She and I will curl up together and watch *Casualty*.'

Craig opened the passenger door and waited for Denise to climb in. She was reminded of the last time she'd done this, and how things had changed since then. He walked round to the driver's side. The silence between them was deafening. Denise knew she had to say something. She turned to him and spoke nervously.

'Speaking of 'not even married', you forgot to mention you were engaged.' She couldn't help herself, and the feeling of anger and frustration overflowed. 'If I'd known about Cynthia . . . '

Would it really have made a difference? How would she not want to hold him whenever he was near? That would be impossible. Being so close to him now made her heart beat faster.

He swung the E-Type into the next lay-by and switched off the engine, then turned to her.

'She's gone back to Lincolnshire. And she isn't my fiancée.' He leaned back in his seat, weariness in his face. 'We were engaged once, in her mind. She's always had the idea she'd marry me one day. Like a schoolgirl crush, only it's always been one-sided — really, it has.'

He turned towards her, all life seeming to drain from him as he spoke.

'How do you let someone down gently when they can't see things as they really are? Jeanie has tried to put her off me dozens of times. Told her she could do better, that kind of thing, how it's not right, to have a one-sided relationship, and she should move on, but she never listens.

'Up until now, it's been easier to stay friends, and keep the peace platonically.' The furrows across his forehead deepened and he looked so sad, Denise

265

wanted to reach over and tell him things would be alright.

After he'd explained in more detail, she asked, 'Does your family know about . . . er . . . the crush?' She wasn't sure if she was pushing her luck, but he looked so sincere, she almost believed him.

'Hah, do they ever? She's round there all the time; the crush has turned into an obsession. Cynthia never stops talking about when she will move in there, to the family home, with me, and trying to talk wedding plans with my mother, who has also tried letting her down gently and explaining how it is.' He let out a long sigh.

'I think we're all too soft. Your note seemed to get through to her, though — now she's gone, after calling me a few choice names, and she's not far wrong.

'She needed telling long ago, but she's quite sensitive — not that it shows, but she is deep down. It would have been kinder to rant and bawl, but that's just not me.' He smiled. 'Now haven't we got a haunting to go to? Ghosts and ghouls wait for no-one.' He re-started the car, looked more relaxed than he had done for quite a while.

* * *

The huge car park to the side of the factory was already beginning to fill up. A group with all kinds of strange equipment and video cameras were organising everyone to help with carrying different items in through the entrance.

'Looks like they need some help.' Craig locked the car and joined the handful of people taking the ghost-busting paraphernalia into the old factory.

'It's the weirdest feeling coming back in.' Maud linked arms with Denise. 'You had a ride in the Jag — that's lovely. Time he moved on from that girl — it's all been such a worry for his mum.'

Of course — Maud was Craig's mother's friend, so she must know all about the Cynthia saga — just as Jeanie did. No wonder she had tried to tell Denise he wasn't available. She knew it would rock the boat.

Denise recalled the moment Cynthia had turned up in the shop, waving her note around. Craig didn't look anything like a man who was in love. She had to believe him, and their moments together in London had been real — she knew that. It was as if electricity fizzed between them every time they came close. He must have felt it.

The ghost-busters had a plan. First of all, the entire group sat around a huge old work table, and chatted about the reasons they were here. The builders had felt a presence, and wanted to know more. Maud wanted to have another look around her old workplace.

'I came to keep Denise company,' Beulah said, but gave her a knowing smile when she saw how close to Craig she was sitting.

Everyone was placed in pairs — Denise with Craig, Maud with a builder named Stan, and Beulah and Tony were huddled so close they didn't take much notice of anyone else.

Mrs Struthers, Beulah's mother, was listening intently as the main man in the ghost watch team was explaining how many different kinds of apparitions may show themselves.

'There are orbs, of course, which we'll capture on video. Sand trays where some spirits like to write messages. We'll have a few groups of us roaming round and making notes as well, and then we'll meet back here in, say, an hour?'

They all nodded and drifted into their designated positions.

Craig and Denise were exploring the upper level of the hat factory, where they had been sent to film orbs, when he pulled her to one side.

'You do believe what I was telling you

earlier? It's been like having a weight across my shoulders. Then when you walked into my office, looking for a job,' he closed his eyes momentarily, 'angels sang and bells rang.' He looked sheepish. 'Now you think I'm being corny. It's the only way to describe it.' He traced his hand along her cheek, the way he'd done in the Savoy.

Denise quivered, but she didn't want to simply say, 'That's alright then,' and fall into his arms.

'What did she expect — to get married and have a family?' She wanted to know more about his childhood crush who seemed to have prevented him from having a proper relationship.

'She wanted to buy me, with her daddy's money. We were going to have a shop, be joint partners — again, all in her mind.'

'But surely you could have told her? An opportunity must have come up.' Denise wondered how he had failed to stop the obsession building up to massive proportions. 'You're your own man. Is that why you stayed over after the weekend in Lincolnshire . . . and the damage?'

He nodded. 'One of her tantrums, and she took it out on the Jag. She tried all ways to keep me in Grantham, and nearby, but I've explained to her, I'm here now. My life changed with my grandma's inheritance. It gave me the chance to make a fresh start — only it's funny how the past follows you around.

'But she knows now. This is my home; I can't keep running back there, trying to keep everyone happy.' He reached over and pushed a strand of her hair behind her ear. 'Cynthia understands now, even though it took a while.'

'Can we not mention her name again? It's the here and now I'm interested in.'

He tilted his head to be on a level with Denise's, so that his lips were an inch from hers.

'You know when you meet that someone special, and words don't seem to matter?' His eyes locked onto hers. They were totally unaware of the dozens of orbs whizzing around behind them.

'I was about to say, it's dark and I'm getting cold . . . but I do know what you mean.' She leaned forward and almost brushed his lips with her own.

'Hold on tight to me, I'll keep you warm, and don't be afraid of the . . . ' Before he could finish what he was saying, their lips met and they melted into each other's arms, then locked together as one. They kissed for what seemed like forever, and Denise knew there was no denying it — she was deeply in love.

14

An almighty bang and thump, followed by a scream, coming from somewhere along the corridor prised the lovers apart. Craig grabbed the video equipment and clasped Denise's hand.

'Whatever it is, we'd better try and get it on film.' His lips lingered on hers. 'Far too distracting being paired with you. Come on.'

She loved the way he entwined his fingers around hers. Like two jigsaw pieces slotting together, it felt as if they were used to doing this hand-holding thing quite often, and from the noises they'd heard, she was glad to have him close by.

They stumbled over some old boxes, and Craig pushed open the door leading to the next room.

'Maud! It's you.'

She and Stanley were mid-embrace.

'Oh, it's alright. Stan was only comforting me. We thought we saw a shape, up in the corner.'

He coughed and Maud dusted herself down.

'We had the same kind of experience back there.' Craig drew Denise towards him and circled her waist with his arms, wrapping them tightly round her. The occasion seemed to bring out the macho in the men.

'What's that over there?' Denise untangled herself and walked over to where she'd spotted an old book on the windowsill. She took a closer look. The full moon cast a wide beam through the high windows and across the shelf, giving the old building an eerie atmosphere.

'An order book, dating back to the mid-seventies.' She flicked through it and handed it to Maud. 'Would you have worked here then?'

She was nodding. 'Yes, and it was Mr Pinkerton who worked in this room, I swear he was sitting there, smiling at me.' As her voice wobbled, Stanley put his arms round her.

'He wouldn't want to hurt you and we've probably disturbed him from years of peace and quiet.' The jolly builder peered into the recess of the former office. 'It's up here where the noises have been coming from mostly, while we've been doing repairs.'

'What's going to happen to the old building? Flats, did we read in the paper?' Denise turned to where Stanley was poking a torch into a built-in cupboard. He turned round.

'Originally, but there's been a change of plan now.' He joined the others and ruffled his hair to remove some dust and cobwebs. 'The council have combined forces with historians — there's one downstairs, and he can tell you more about it. Anyway, the Lottery grant is big enough to make it into a museum to local industry. Hats, of course, and there used to be a knitwear factory in town, didn't there?' He looked at Maud. 'They think it will be more beneficial, being in the town, to have it as a tourist attraction.'

'That's right, shoes, boots, hosiery; you name it, Mullsey made it.' Maud nodded. 'You'd have bought your tights from Mullsey, wouldn't you?' She smiled at Craig.

'For the market stall,' he added pointedly, 'and no jokes about me being in tights, thank you. You're talking about before my time, though. I used to go over to the Leicester side for my tights . . . to sell.' When he gave her hand a squeeze, Denise felt warm and fuzzy all over and tried not to laugh at the image he'd conjured up.

'Of course, they'll still be having the craft shops, and there's talk of having living accommodation above them,' the builder explained.

Denise didn't let on she'd applied for one. There was no point until she knew for sure.

'Should be a real asset to the town and it's great to be able to look around it.' Stanley draped his arm round

Maud's shoulder. 'You warm enough, love? I thought you gave a little tremble just then. Have my jacket if you're cold.' Without waiting for a reply, the builder took off his padded coat and made sure Maud was cosy. 'Can't have a lovely lady like you getting a chill now, can we?'

As soon as he'd mentioned the word 'chill' a cold breeze drifted through the room and a creaking sound broke up their chatter.

'Get the filming going,' Stanley hissed. 'Something might show on camera that we can't see with the naked eye.'

Torches flashed and video cameras caught some odd-looking flying things, even if they might only be insects that were not happy being invaded at this time of night.

When they left the top floor, Maud looked back and shivered.

'I swear that was him in there.' She pulled Stanley's jacket round her shoulders and made her way stealthily back downstairs with the others.

The local historian was sitting with two more builders, and Denise couldn't help overhearing their conversation about the shops.

'How many will there be?' She pulled up a chair and took the chance to ask while Craig had gone to fetch some more food supplies from the boot of his car.

'Only the three. I think one of them is taken already, and plenty of offers on the others.' He smiled. Denise froze and hoped he didn't realise she was one of those people. She wanted to change the subject from shops in case Craig came back in the middle of the conversation. She didn't want him to think she was being deceitful.

'It's going to be a real feature . . . cobbled street as visitors approach, and lots of the original machinery and photos from when the factory first opened. There's talk of a museum café as well, serving old-fashioned food. The canal heritage will be included, and the link to Boadicea and her battle with the Romans.'

Now the historian was on his specialist subject, facts coming thick and fast. Denise was sure that he'd be a permanent fixture once the museum was open, as a tour guide. Or if not, he should be.

In between taking a tour of the old factory, and eating sandwiches, emptying flasks of tea, hot chocolate and coffee, the band of psychic hunters had a fascinating time. At around two o'clock in the morning, due to draughts and lots of activity having being recorded, that the ghost-busters called it a night.

'We'll be having a follow-up meeting, to go over things if anyone wants to come.' Peter Amperton, chief ghost-buster, was talking mostly to Beulah's mother. 'We'll be meeting in the Owl and Compass next weekend if that suits.'

From the look on Mrs Struthers' face, it did suit perfectly, and they all parted ways.

On the way home, Craig pulled into the same gateway as he had stopped in hours earlier.

'I'll give you a hand moving the hats to the shop. Tomorrow, if you like.' He leaned in close.

'You mean the tomorrow that's now today?' She smiled. 'Make it later on; I'll be knocked out before long.' Wishing she'd said something more romantic, she could have kicked herself. Here she was with the man of her dreams and all she could say was the most idiotic thing ever.

'My kisses have that effect on you?' He raised one eyebrow and tilted her chin.

Before long she was in a whirlwind of his kisses once again. It felt as if she were flying away on a magic carpet to somewhere she'd never been, and wanted to stay forever. Only when their lips parted, he held her close and whispered, 'I've never been so happy.' He caressed her fairy necklace and then kissed the tip of her nose. 'Now I'll get you home before your landlady sends out a search party.'

★ ★ ★

After such an eventful night, Denise couldn't sleep, so she got up early to organise her shed.

Lace, in pastel colours and bolder shades, was wound round stiff card and stacked neatly on the top shelf. She used that quite frequently in the children's hats, for christenings and weddings. A vase filled with varying lengths and hues of feathers stood in the corner. Her supply of hat boxes was bursting off a lower shelf, and she had a stack of basic hats ready for decorating. Baskets of buttons, all shapes and sizes, were on a level with the workbench, and she tidied up the papers and shoved her latest orders into the small drawer she used as a filing cabinet.

Cinders was curled up in a box on top of an old jumper, under the bench waiting for a trail of ribbon to dangle down, which it invariably did. The whole workshop was a riot of colour and textures with hats piled high everywhere you looked. That was where Craig found her later that morning, her hair tied back with a ragged flowery bow and her embroidered jeans cut off just below the knee.

'Hi! I've been sorting out the most popular ones.' Why did she feel shy, when last night they'd spent more time kissing than ghost hunting?

Denise watched him look around at the higgledy-piggledy random semi-organisation that only she knew how to achieve.

For once, Craig let someone else tell him what was needed and which items would sell best. The tension had gone from his brow, and he seemed to enjoy being told what to do. Denise felt a buzz of excitement seeing how much he respected what she'd achieved so far.

'There are a few more in the house,' Denise informed Craig, then skipped across the lawn, and nipped into the kitchen where Sadie was preparing the roast pork and stuffing lunch.

'I meant to say to you, there's plenty here if he wants to stay.' She nodded towards the bottom of the garden where Craig was piling up boxes. 'And Beulah rang. She's coming round to give you a hand as well.'

Always happy when she was cooking for a crowd, Sadie slid an apple crumble into the oven.

'Oh, that's good. We'd never get all those hat boxes in Craig's car.' Denise dipped her finger into a bowl of apple sauce and tasted it.

'Mmm, just testing. It passes,' she teased.

'Cheeky monkey. Something's perked you up today, and if I'm not mistaken, he's walking this way. Ask him to stay for lunch.'

Knowing Sadie wouldn't keep quiet until she knew how many plates to put to warm, Denise leaned out of the back door and called to Craig.

'Sadie says, would you like to stay for lunch?'

Peering round a stack of hat boxes as he passed, Craig's eyes homed in on Sadie arranging roast potatoes and stuffing balls on a huge plate.

'Well, now I've seen what's on offer, how could I refuse?' He gave a hint of a wink towards Denise, and carried the boxes to his car. 'I'll pop along to the shop with these, and be back in about half an hour. You made a note of everything I've had so far?' He checked with Denise, who had come out to help him load up.

'Yes, and there are some different ones in the house — we can leave those until after lunch.' She passed him the colourful boxes decorated with butterflies and spots and stripes.

'They'll brighten the window, and hopefully you'll soon be getting a hat factory of your own going. Let's hope our visit to the actual place rubbed off a bit.' He caught her hand and brushed her fingertips against his lips. 'Back in a while, and if Sadie wants to dish up, don't wait for me.' He started the car and leaned out of the window.

'You're joking — she'll want to wait until you get back. It's a proper sit-at-the-table affair with Sadie on a Sunday. The diet starts tomorrow.' Denise laughed and patted her middle.

★   ★   ★

The thud as a collection of mail hit the mat had Denise running to see if anything interesting had arrived. The post came early on Mondays. She scooped up Cinders, along with the letters and ripped open an envelope with her name on.

'Yes, I've passed . . . ' She danced into the kitchen waving the envelope. 'Well, not exactly top marks — ' she took a closer look and pulled a face, only for a second — 'but enough to say I'm now qualified in textiles and design. Woo hoo!'

Plonking herself down on a kitchen

chair to take a breath, Denise looked apprehensively at the other envelope marked *Mullsey Council*.

'Oh no, I can't open that one. Will you?' She handed the offending item to her landlady who'd been in the middle of scraping mud off her gardening boots. As she put the brush down, Cinders pounced on it.

'That's good news, love. Now you'll be able to get the certificate framed to go in the shed. Or Craig might let you put it up in his shop.'

She put her boots, and the newspaper they stood on, to one side.

'Now let's have a look at this, then?' Giving her hands a wash and wipe, Sadie slotted her crinkled vegetable knife along the seal of the envelope, then pulled out the letter.

'*Dear Miss Gambon, it is with great pleasure that I am able to inform you that you have . . .* ' She read on in silence . . . 'Oh, heck, you've only gone and got the shop.' Sadie stood open-mouthed before throwing her arms up and shouting, 'You've got your shop!' She threw her arms round Denise and waltzed her round the kitchen, then stopped to wipe away a tear.

'And you never said a word to Craig, did you? I didn't either. Best tell him nearer the time, eh?'

Denise nodded; Sadie had the same thoughts as she did.

If he thought she was branching out on her own, he might not have been so quick and helpful with letting her have a display in his shop. Or was it more that she didn't want to hurt his feelings — worse still, leave him alone, available for any old flame to turn up and whisk him away?

Beulah had also passed her exams, and came round for coffee and cake to celebrate.

'Seems kind of strange that we've finished with all our studies, doesn't it? Not sure what I'm going to do. I can give you a hand when the time comes to get the shop ready.'

She was over the moon when she

heard her friend's news.

'But what will happen about your shifts at Something Special when you need to be in your own shop full-time?' she asked.

'Hopefully I'll branch into it gradually, but Craig'll have to get someone in my place.'

Denise looked at Beulah who was examining her nails, not in a vain way, but in a manner that was saying, *look no further*.

Denise laughed out loud.

'Of course. You'd be ideal, and you know the ladies already. Just don't mention anything about me leaving yet — it'll sound better coming from me. I'm dreading telling him, though.'

Beulah smiled. 'Stop fretting; you'll have enough to think about. I can come with you, though, when you need to get more supplies. You spoke about going to Nottingham the other day. Did you get the postcode of the warehouse?'

Denise nodded and reached for her notebook. With a friend like Beulah, a landlady like Sadie and a man whose kisses tasted of honey, no wonder she had a permanent smile on her lips.

★ ★ ★

'The offer of a weekend in Paris is still open. I'd really like you to go; you'd get a feel of what else is in the market place regarding fashions.' Craig held up his hand before Denise could protest. 'I know, you have your own ideas — look.' He gestured towards the shop window, filled with hats. 'They're amazing — and selling well, too.'

He watched Denise fill up a rack with Fair Isle socks. 'It's been a great help with all the Royal events over the past year. The Queen's ninetieth birthday celebrations have given the hat and dress trade a massive boost and if Kate's wearing it on Monday, the shops have sold out by Friday.' He smiled. 'You should send her some samples.'

Now Denise knew he'd gone over the top.

'I'd love to go to Paris with you — but sending samples to the Duchess?'

She made a face and pulled a box marked *Autumn Specials* from by the door. There was a real flavour of Fair Isle, and tartan was making a comeback, from the look of the latest autumn stock that had recently arrived.

It seemed strange, as there was a heatwave going on, and the gardens were looking spectacular due to a regular downpour of balmy rain during the night.

Denise took note of the tweedy textures and planned to make hats to go with the fabrics on show in Craig's shop. She still hadn't mentioned having her own shop. On the way to Paris might be a good time — when they were alone.

* * *

Two weeks later, after the contract had been signed, Joe was on hand with his van and Beulah arrived with her car to transport the smaller items like buckles, lace and buttons. Sadie was already at the shop with her mop, bucket and feather duster. Denise had told her not to worry too much, but Sadie wanted to make sure it had been scrubbed to within an inch of its life.

The sign-writer had arrived on time, at nine o'clock and fitted the cream sign with calligraphy spelling out *Mullsey Hats* in bottle-green letters. Beulah stood back and took a picture.

'For your website and blog.' She opened her eyes wide. 'You need to tell you-know-who.'

Yes, she knew she ought to be saying something, and she would . . . on the way to Paris. Hers was the corner shop — the largest of the three. Another one was an artist's studio, with local landscapes — bluebell woods, barges along the canal, Mullsey church and the market square, to name a few of the scenes for sale. The third was a bookshop. On the door someone had posted an advertisement telling of a writers' group to be held once a month in the shop.

As the sun cast its rays across the cobbles, Denise had a feeling she was going to be happy here, running her own business — and doing what she liked best. Shielding her eyes from the September sun, she looked up. Underneath the name of the shop, in smaller letters, she read *Miss Denise Gambon — Milliner*.

★ ★ ★

They flew from East Midlands Airport, and arrived in Beauvais Tillé airport a little less than an hour later. It was during the flight, when Craig had a whisky in one hand and the in-flight magazine in the other, that she'd told him.

'I've got my own shop.'

His reaction wasn't what she'd been expecting. He didn't look up from the magazine.

'Of course you have. You'd be an idiot not to.' He threw the magazine to one side, drank the whisky down in one, and turned to face her.

'So does this mean we're business rivals?'

The crinkles around his eyes and the crooked smile threw her slightly. He was making fun. From the look on his face it must be the most hilarious thing he'd heard in a long time.

'I wanted to tell you sooner, of course, but it's only recently I found out myself, and what with stocking it and ordering more materials — '

He put his finger up to her lips.

'You don't have to make excuses. You thought I'd fling my dummy out of the pram? Or more likely, your hats out onto the pavement, is that it?' She saw the frown appear. 'You don't know me very well, then. Please don't humour me and treat me like some drippy kid. You weren't going to get a bigger shed, were you?'

He smiled with a world-weary air,

and an overwhelming sadness drifted between them. Denise left him to his thoughts.

★ ★ ★

It was the evening of the fashion show, and almost time for them to leave the hotel. Denise wore a black and white Chanel outfit — found in a charity shop in Birmingham when she and Beulah had been out on a shopping spree. It made her feel really special, so stuff Craig Spencer. If he didn't want to be treated like a drippy kid, why act like one?

Her own creation, a tiny black hat with netting attached to the brim, a curled swirl rising from it and trimmed with black and white bow, gave her added height and a feeling of being a woman in charge of her own destiny. The most expensive items she wore were the silk stockings.

Before coming here, she had some wild idea of making love at every opportunity. Now it was definitely a business trip, seeing as she'd laid her cards on the table, so to speak.

Craig was dressed in a black suit with a crisp white shirt. She smiled as they made their way to the taxi rank. If they'd planned it, they couldn't have looked more like a matching pair. He held his arm out for her to link in with him.

Always gentlemanly, he was more distant now than ever. That suited her fine; she would have to get used to not being the Saturday girl now. She climbed into the taxi and glanced out of the window.

Paris was alive with colour and all the women were so stylish, Denise was soon in awe. She tingled in anticipation and turned to Craig.

'I'm so happy to be here . . . with you.' She gave him a wide smile and squeezed his hand. 'Thanks for asking me.'

'Don't be crazy. I knew you'd love it. Wait until the show starts.' His eyes were dazzling blue with a hint of mischief. 'You look stunning tonight.'

He pulled her hand to his lips and kissed her fingertips. He was quieter than normal, but Denise put that down to the news of her setting up on her own. At least the silence was broken now and she looked forward to the show.

Music thumped out from speakers around the huge hall, and strong perfumes and aromas of expensive aftershave wafted past her as immaculately dressed people mingled and found seats. They were half way back from the catwalk, or runway she heard people calling it.

Denise felt like a stunned rabbit, taking in the luxurious surroundings and opulent furnishings. Then the show began.

Sultry models strutted and pouted, and she began to relax and enjoy the performance. Next up came a cheerful eccentric tune, about keeping young and beautiful . . . and then came the hats. Oh, joy! She turned to Craig.

'Amazing, you were right, there are hats . . .' She gasped and leaned forward on her chair.

A deep purple with mallard feather, the same as hers — followed by a wide cerise brim, with matching flowers, three in a cluster — like hers. Her face dropped. Then a tall blonde model with a trilby set at a jaunty angle, exactly the same as Beulah's . . .

Denise felt sick. This was a replica of her collection. Not only that — all of these hats were the ones from Craig's window.

She turned towards him, heart hammering as if it might break free from her chest.

'You've stolen my designs!' Her hands and lips were shaking so badly, she could hardly speak. Tears sprang to her eyelids and she swallowed hard. 'How could you?'

She'd seen enough. Grappling with her handbag, she pushed past everyone on the row of chairs between her and the gangway. Then she began to run, and run.

Vaguely aware of his voice somewhere behind her, she didn't stop running until she escaped from the Carrousel du Louvre.

Stopping for breath, Denise bent double with the pain. She heard that familiar voice.

'Listen, to me. Come back in, Denise — the show has only just begun.' He reached for her hand, but she shrugged him off.

'Don't touch me. I hate you, Craig Spencer.'

Amid a flood of tears, Denise escaped into the crowd. She knew he wasn't bothering to follow, and she was glad.

15

Back at the hotel, Denise called a taxi to the airport then switched her phone off without bothering to look at it. She threw her belongings into her bag.

'Take me to the nearest airport, please.' On arrival, she booked the next available plane home. The journey went by in a blur. When she eventually arrived back in Mullsey, and home to Sadie's cottage, she could have collapsed from the disappointment of it all.

Denise dumped her bag at the foot of the stairs and slumped into the nearest chair.

'I can't believe he'd do such a horrible thing.' She looked up at Sadie, standing open-mouthed. 'My hats — he *stole* them. I hadn't a clue until they were there on show, being paraded in front of me. I didn't twig on at first, and there was me thinking they were the same as mine. That's because they *were* mine.

'No wonder he was so keen to get his hands on them. I'm glad to be home. It was a stupid idea to go there with him in the first place.'

Sadie bustled round and made something to eat, but Denise wasn't hungry. She went straight to bed and in between bursts of crying and thumping her pillow, slept for ten hours. Cinders sat at the foot of her bed, looking at her uncomprehendingly with big blue eyes.

Sadie brought in a jug of water with lemon slices and ice that rattled as she set it down.

'Now . . . This has gone on long enough.'

Denise lifted herself up onto her elbow and gave a wan smile.

'Thanks for the drink, and you're right. I just felt washed out — sorry.'

'Nobody's worth all these tears, love. At least have a drink of water.'

Sadie collected an empty tea cup and then left.

'She's right, Cinders.' The grey kitten that was not so small anymore arched her back and lifted her tail into a high brush in agreement. 'Let's show him, shall we? There's work to be done.'

Pushing back the curtains and pulling on her comfy jeans and a jumper, Denise washed her face and tied her hair up into a top knot, then secured it with a flower hair accessory. 'Flipping heck, I'm hungry, though.'

She looked at herself in the mirror. Her eyes had bags underneath big enough to hold a week's luggage, and her skin looked dreadful.

In her drawer she found some tinted moisturiser, and a lipstick. Then a flick of mascara and creamy blue on her eyelids. She felt a bit more human, if still lacklustre.

She slumped on the bed to pull on her worn-out trainers, then made her way downstairs, Cinders weaving in between her feet at every step.

'Ah, at last. I thought you'd gone to bed for the week.' Sadie was rustling up scrambled eggs and bacon, and never before had Denise looked forward to a breakfast so much.

'It's all over, Sadie. No more job for me at Something Special and no more Mr Craig Spencer round for Sunday lunch either. From now on it's me and my best friends only.'

She scooped Cinders up with one hand, and draped her other arm round Sadie's shoulder.

'You did mention, about the hats, yes. I think you should have stayed, asked him to tell you what his game was.' Sadie looked upset. 'He was always such a gentleman, and he enjoyed my cooking.' Then she looked even more deflated.

'I can't say that I ever really knew him, can I? Apart from working in the shop. First there's Jeanie telling me he's not available, then up turns a long-lost fiancée, and then he sits me down at a fashion show where my hats are paraded out in front of me and he thinks it's a good game. Well, I don't.' Denise's shoulders slumped.

'Eat some breakfast. He'll be in touch. He'll have a perfect explanation and then you'll say . . . '

Denise began eating hungrily. 'I hope you're right, but I don't see how there can be. Breakfast is wonderful, thanks. Can we change the subject now, Sadie? I've got a shop to sort out.'

* * *

The ground floor of her shop had plenty of room for displaying the hats and haberdashery accessories. A staircase towards the back led to the next level where she'd made an office at the front near the window, and furnished the other side of the room to form a bedsit. The furniture had been picked up from charity shops and with Beulah helping by chalk-painting the wooden parts in duck egg blue, it was now quite cosy.

Not that she'd moved in full time — Sadie's cooking and company were far too welcoming for that. Often during the week, she stayed overnight if she'd become engrossed in her designs.

There was a kettle and microwave, a really small fridge that had been on special offer at the supermarket and a cupboard with a couple of shelves above for storing a few essentials.

Tonight she was having beans on toast for speed as she wanted to carry on sketching. Denise found that time spent on her design work helped block out the emptiness that would creep up to haunt her when she least expected it.

During those times, she wondered if she'd get by without ever feeling that butterfly flip inside when a certain man came near. The perfect remedy to forget — because she had to forget about him — was to design another hat. The pile of new designs was mounting.

Not that she wanted to know how he was or what he was doing. If he cared, he'd phone or text or . . . something.

Craig couldn't sleep, eat or function properly. His big surprise had turned out a disaster. The woman he loved was supposed to turn to him and gasp at his ingenious plan — to showcase the most stylish hats he'd seen on the fashion circuit — to launch her career, and then they were supposed to celebrate together afterwards.

He'd planned to walk with her along the Champs-Elysées, drink whipped hot chocolate in tall glasses from a street café and eat delicious pastries. Later, they should have been watching the lights twinkle as the Eiffel Tower came to life after dark. He'd even had the mad notion . . . no, what was he thinking? She'd made it plain how little she thought of him, and every time he recalled the hurt on her face as she left, he knew she needed time. He was a patient man.

Being on the premises made it easier for her to keep track of who wanted what, and now she was ordering felt direct from the manufacturers in Nottingham and Bradford. She didn't have time for dyeing her own materials as she had in the shed, and the vintage range was taking off in a way she could never have dreamed of.

'Would you like me to measure you for size?' Denise pointed to the hat the latest customer was holding, made from tapestry fabric with a wide rust-coloured ribbon sash. It was from her 1920s range.

'Actually, it fits alright. What do you think?'

She donned the hat and looked into the huge round mirror on the back wall.

Immediately the transformation took place. From being a plain, slightly dowdy individual, it was as if the woman had stepped into a role in an Agatha Christie murder mystery. Denise noticed the tilt to her head and slight pout. Her customer became a sultry siren with one raised eyebrow.

She smiled and nodded to her in the mirror. Without a doubt, she knew she had a sale.

* * *

Blue and white lights decorated Mullsey High Street, throwing a sparkling halo over the town. Diwali evening had brought out crowds to watch the street dancing and Festival of Lights. It happened to coincide with Hallowe'en weekend as well.

A firework display was scheduled for Mullsey recreation field later on into the night. Some of the shops and eating places were open, and Denise had decided to open her shop in readiness for any browsers or window shoppers. Already there was a small crowd milling around.

The taxi had taken the route through the main street. She could see that a stage was erected on the market square and a play was being performed. The main festivals took place in Leicester and Birmingham, but bit by bit, the surrounding towns had begun to hold celebrations of their own. Her taxi took her up towards the canal bridge to where Mullsey Hats stood on the corner, next to the others in the row below the Hat Factory Museum.

She never failed to tingle with pride when she saw the Victorian-style windows with tiny square panes. She'd decorated them with fairy lanterns in readiness for the festival, and they would stay there for the build-up to Christmas, and into New Year, as her displays around them changed.

Quite a few of her regular customers had taken advantage of her new hat hire service. It wasn't something she'd planned to do, but the idea was inspired by several people asking for something special for one night only. It was profitable, too.

She'd popped in to see Sadie, who as

if by magic had produced a delicious soup.

'I always keep something in the freezer. You're like a Cheshire cat, appearing and disappearing, and I never know when,' Sadie scolded, but she wore a smile that told Denise she was only joking.

Turning the key in the shop door, Denise entered and glanced round at her display of hats, before reaching behind the counter to switch on the window lights. Next she flicked the heating switch on.

It was a cold night, but that hadn't put people off coming in to town. The museum was open, the book shop and art centre as well. She'd taken most of the day off, and now as evening approached, she was fresh and eager to welcome people. Whether they bought anything or not, it was an opportunity to chat and maybe take some orders for the festive season and beyond.

The museum had laid on games for children. They had to seek out clues and then follow a trail, and if the shrieks of laughter were any measure, they were enjoying themselves. Organisers had asked if she wanted to be involved in the game and let them traipse through her shop, but she'd politely said she'd pass. She was just not in the mood for that kind of thing at the moment.

It was around half-past eight when her shop bell began to chime.

'Is it alright if we just have a look?'

The two ladies looked around as if they'd found Aladdin's cave and they ended up buying a maroon cloche and a checked waterproof gathered hat — for every day and 'when I'm walking the dog,' the checked hat lady had said.

The maroon one was for her friend's church coffee mornings to go with her new jacket.

The evening drew a steady flow of customers and Denise took orders as well as selling more than a dozen hats. She was delighted with the outcome and ready for bed when the church clock struck ten o'clock and everyone headed off in the direction of the recreation ground. The firework display would round off the eventful evening.

Gathering up Cinders from her usual spot under the counter, Denise locked the shop door, bolted it, then pulled the blinds. Checking that the side door was locked and bolted as well, she made her way upstairs where she mixed a hot chocolate and went through her latest designs.

Every time she had thoughts of Craig, she'd sketched a new hat design. Her pile of new ideas was quite high and growing by the day. Even though she probably wouldn't make half of them, she had an awful lot to choose from — over a hundred if she'd been counting.

The crackle and bangs from the firework display drifted across the town. From her window she could hear distant cries of 'Oh' and 'Ah' from families having fun.

She pushed aside thoughts of how

families, and having fun, seemed to be things that had escaped her. They were what other people did. Still, she was happy with her business. It was what she'd set out to do: to be independent financially.

She looked at Cinders who was pacing back and forth by the door, mewing as if she wanted to go out. Next she was scratching at the door, and then circling her feet and mewing.

'What's the matter, puss? You've been out earlier. It's not like you.' Cinders stared at the door and hissed, then meowed and scratched some more then fixed her blue eyes on to Denise as if trying really hard to tell her something. 'What?'

Looking out of the window, Denise saw the glow from another rocket that soared and crackled, showering Mullsey town with a rainbow of sparkles. She could almost smell the smoke — yet she was the other side of the town.

Cinders was making more of a yowling than mewing sound now.

Denise decided to investigate what was bothering her on the other side of the door. As she opened it, the unmistakable smell of smoke drifted towards her.

This wasn't anything to do with the fireworks — unless some of the village kids had shoved a banger through her letterbox and run off.

A quick glance down the stairs caused her to gasp. Quickly pulling her jumper over her face, she grabbed Cinders and bolted back into the room at the top. It wasn't safe to go down; she'd smelled acrid burning and amid the swirl of smoke, she saw red flaming tongues licking at her possessions in the shop below.

Her first thought was . . . *The hats!* Then she grabbed her mobile to ring 999. Drat, she had a flat battery . . . and her landline was downstairs.

She gave a hefty shove on the sash window. Leaning out, Denise hollered with all of her breath.

'Help! There's a fire. I'm trapped.'

She looked down and wondered if

she dared jump. No — too far. She wasn't feeling at all brave, and now she began to breathe more rapidly, swallowing hard and trying not to go into a panic attack. Clutching Cinders to her chest, she shouted again, 'Help me, please.'

Denise could only hope that someone in the museum or the other shops might hear, or smell the smoke that was building up now. Almost everyone was over the other side of town. She could see from leaning out that smoke was billowing out of the bottom window.

Frantically she looked around for anything to use as a rope, to tie on the door handle and shin down. That's what they did in films, wasn't it? However all she could find to hand was some lace and flimsy ribbon on her desk — hardly the stuff of heroic escapes from a burning building.

She heard shouts from below.

'We've rung the fire brigade — they should be here any minute.' Denise recognised a woman from the museum.

Taking a gulp of fresh air and shouting down, 'Thank you,' Denise saw a flash of blue shooting round the corner of Hatters Walk. She gasped as the E-Type Jag skidded to a halt, only just short of the cast iron bollards that prevented traffic from going any further up the road outside her shop.

Craig jumped from his seat and grappled for something beside him. It was his long charcoal-grey overcoat — he'd taken it to London, and looked gorgeous in it. He shouted up to her.

'Hold on, I'll be there in two minutes. Stay by the window and don't open the door.'

He shrugged on his overcoat, and pulled a balaclava-type hat over his face.

'Hold on there, love. I can't believe it — he's coming in.' The lady from the museum was looking on in horror, her hands to her face as crashing noises came from below. 'He's smashed the door in already. It's dangerous, he should wait! They'll be here soon, we've raised the alarm.'

'Thank you,' she croaked, but saw the fear on the faces of the people standing by.

Please keep him safe, don't let him burn. She could only hope and pray that Craig was able to find a way through. Clutching onto her pendant, the one he bought her from Covent Garden, she slowly counted seconds.

The door to the office burst open, then closed immediately. Craig looked like a masked intruder. Unable to speak, Denise clutched Cinders to her chest and stood still for fear of collapsing like a babbling idiot into his arms.

He rushed towards the sink and soaked several sheets of kitchen roll in cold water.

'Right, take a lungful of air from the window first.' She noticed him wipe his face with the towelling, and then soak the balaclava and quickly squeeze it out before replacing it. Next he drenched a tea towel in water, and draped it over her head.

'Hold my hand and follow me. Keep a tight hold on the cat. Don't move that towel, keep it over your face to help you breathe, and don't stop.'

Without another word, he pulled her towards the door. If ever she'd been in a life-or-death situation, this was it and if there was anyone she'd want with her at a time like this, Craig was the man.

Smoke and flames were gathering force at the foot of the stairs. Denise hadn't a clue how he'd got up those stairs without getting burned. His coat must have protected him a bit, but she wasn't sure they'd get through alive. Next minute he'd whisked her into his arms. She felt the strength and power of his body as he took great running strides, and then stumbled down the bottom few stairs. She buried her face into the wet cloth and gulped as he'd told her. For a split second she wondered whether they'd make it as a roaring sound surrounded them and the acrid burning reached the back of her throat.

The heat was overpowering and she knew without seeing that the whole shop was ablaze. Spitting debris was falling on them as he charged through the inferno. Terrified, Cinders sank needle-sharp claws into her chest. Craig leaned his body into hers, keeping her safe as he ran like a gladiator through the burning building and out to the safety of the cobbled yard.

The fire engine screamed into Hatter's Walk. Through streaming eyes that stung and hurt more than she'd ever known, Denise gazed through the woollen spaces into the deep blue eyes of her rescuer. He tugged off his unconventional protective headgear.

From what seemed like very far away, Denise heard the clamour as a fire crew rushed to mobilise the water hoses then trained them on the shop. One came over to Craig and Denise.

'Is there anyone else in the building? We had a call from the curator at the museum. We came as fast as we could. Looks as if she's had a lucky escape . . . oh, and mate, anytime you want a job, give us a call, but don't do it again without the proper gear.'

Craig coughed, breathed deeply and turned towards Denise.

'I should have asked you about the show — it was meant to be a surprise. You've had over a hundred orders through Something Special already. It was meant to launch your career . . . only you didn't need my help.'

He glanced towards the shop, the flames succumbing to the hoses.

'You did that for me?' Denise gasped. 'And tonight . . . how did you know, about the fire?'

Denise frowned, and checked that Cinders, saucer-eyed and still firmly attached to her by twenty small claws, was able to breathe.

'Jeanie called me. She was in a right state. Cynthia had rung her, bragging that you wouldn't be getting in her way any longer and that you'd soon be up in flames. She'd been drinking, according to what Jeanie said, and raging about our trip to Paris.'

The man she'd always loved placed his mouth on hers gently, then brushed her hair from her face and threw the soggy cloth to one side.

She kissed him back and then started to say, 'About that weekend in Paris . . . '

He shook his head and placed his index finger gently on her lips.

'As long as you're safe, that's all that matters.'

'She tried to kill me.' Denise's knees buckled. 'But I never set out to steal you from anyone.'

An ambulance had arrived and paramedics were running towards them.

'I've been yours since that day you walked into my life, and I'll make sure Cynthia never comes near you or me ever again, I promise. Arson is a serious offence, that's on top of stalking and harassment. Oh, and damage to my property, and hounding the parents. She's gone too far.'

He only let her go when the ambulance crew led them both to the waiting vehicle. He squeezed her hand tightly, and then flinched. Denise noticed burns on the back of his hands.

'Craig. Can we start afresh?' Then she shook herself. 'What am I saying? I have nothing.' Her lip quivered.

'You've got me, and we'll sort out the shop. Don't worry about anything — we'll work it out.' He looked deep into her eyes as the ambulance drove them away to Mullsey General. 'I want to marry you, Denise.'

That cascade of butterflies was back.

'Yes, Craig. I'll marry you — just in case you're high on smoke inhalation and change your mind tomorrow!' she gulped, and tears escaped.

He stripped off his coat, stuffed the balaclava into his pocket, then threw them on the floor of the ambulance. 'They're no good now, but a small price to pay to save the woman I love.'

'You're wrong — I'll remember them forever. The sight of you tearing through the door, my hero . . . '

Craig's mouth covered hers, and no more words were needed.